August Heat

George Helman

Contents

one | no room at the inn

MAYBE THE TRAVEL exhaustion was getting to me, but I could have sworn that the gray-haired man behind the hotel counter said I didn't have a room reservation.

I had to have a reservation. This was the only hotel on Evergreen Isle, and the ferry back to mainland South Carolina already left for the evening. The only ferry.

This was the perfect example of why I never left New York City. The big apple may have a lingering unpleasant odor and constant traffic noise, but it was predictable. I knew every apartment I toured would be overpriced and undersized. I knew I'd need to watch for dog shit on street corners during my morning commute. But all of its flaws only made me smile. I knew what to expect, and it was home.

When I did travel, I liked going places I could heavily research. Places that had books on tourism and blogs with trusted opinions.

But one place no one had ever written a blog post about?

Evergreen Isle, of course.

I wouldn't have dared to get on that ferry earlier if my job didn't depend on it.

"Sorry, but we're full up," the man repeated. Mark, according to his name tag.

Mark didn't sound sorry at all. In fact, he reminded me a bit of a tropical Santa Claus who'd decided to go on a diet and was miserable about his cookie restriction, so he decided to bring everyone's mood down with him.

"You're not from around these parts, are you?" he asked when I struggled to find the right response to the whole no room at the inn thing.

I bit down on my tongue to keep a cutting remark in. If I were from around these parts, I probably wouldn't be asking for a room, would I?

"Just in town visiting," I replied before pulling out my trusty folder of travel documents and finding the printout of the confirmation email for my stay. "This is a copy of my reservation details. My room was booked over a month ago. Quinn Castle. With the New York Warriors."

Mark lazily took the paper, scanned it for all of a few seconds, and then tossed it back onto the counter. "This is for our sister hotel on Emerald Isle. It's the next island over."

I snatched the paper up, my eyes darting through the words in the email until...yep, there it was. Emerald Isle.

This would not have happened if August Fletcher lived in the sort of place that people wrote blog posts about.

"Are you visiting someone?" Mark pressed, oblivious to my internal panic.

I nodded absently while tucking my good-for-nothing confirmation email back into my folder.

"Yeah?" he questioned. "Who?"

"Pardon?"

I wasn't sure if he'd meant for it to sound like a challenge, as though I'd lie about my reasons for being on the island, but that was definitely what I heard.

"Who are you visiting?"

He over-pronounced the words as if my hearing had been the problem the first time, not his attitude.

"August Fletcher." I looked down at my phone to see if I had any notifications. I didn't. "That is, if he'll respond to my message so I can figure out where to find him."

"The island's not that big," the man chuckled, looking amused for the first time since I'd walked into his beachy hole-in-the-wall resort. "You'll eventually find everything you need to. Besides, Auggie's always in the same spot this time of day." He clucked his tongue. "Shoulda known you were here to see him."

I raised a brow. "Is that so?" I asked, ignoring the last part.

If Mark could help me find August Fletcher, I'd toss out all my previous judgments about him. Suddenly, Mark was my very best friend who'd earned a five-star review of his somewhat dilapidated hotel even though he refused to rent me a room.

"Sunny's." Mark nodded confidently. "I'd bet my last dollar he'll be at the bar."

"And how might I get to Sunny's?" I asked, trying not to let my eagerness shine through too much.

Mark planted his elbows on the counter and leaned forward while using his pen as a pointer stick, gesturing out the window. "If you follow this road back to the main drag, you'll see Sunny's on the left next to the post office."

I nodded, thinking that his directions sounded vague but easy enough. Hopefully Mark wasn't leading me astray. But seeing as I didn't have anyone else to trust and no blog post to reference, I smiled at the tropical Santa.

"Thank you so much!" I grabbed my suitcase by the handle and wheeled it around. "I'll head there now."

"Welcome." Mark seemed pleased with himself, but then he raised a brow. "Good luck with that one."

"Thanks," I laughed before heading out the door.

I'd need all the luck I could get.

Before he'd unexpectedly retired a few months ago, August Fletcher was the Warriors player that all the reporters avoided. Because, well, he avoided them. He made it no secret that he hated dealing with the media, but he was going to have to deal with me whether he liked it or not.

After all, his early retirement was the entire reason I was trucging my suitcase down a shoddy island road to find him while trying not to get sand in my worn leather sandals.

I tipped my head to the sky, welcoming its rays. A fresh breeze skirted over my skin. Yes, the sand in my shoes was uncomfortable. And sure, maybe I'd be sleeping on the beach tonight—miles away from New York City.

But I couldn't deny how good that sun felt.

Maybe spending some of my summer on Evergreen Isle wasn't the worst thing that could have happened to me.

***

AS IT TURNED out, it wasn't hard to find Sunny's once I dragged my luggage into the center of the sleepy beach town.

It wasn't hard to find August, either, being that he was the only ruggedly handsome, chiseled-jaw patron sitting at the bar. His large, muscled form was hard to miss, and I took a deep breath as I dodged half-broken chairs and wobbly tables on my way over to him.

While August had never denied me the chance to interview him, that didn't mean he was necessarily pleasant about it. And I expected him to be even less pleasant today, considering I'd chased him to his hometown.

"You found me."

He said the words without looking at me when I sidled next to him at the bar, and the gruffness of his voice sent a shiver up my spine that had nothing to do with the temperature, which could only be described as sweltering.

Tucking my suitcase under my legs, I centered my tired ass on the barstool and flagged down the bartender. I needed a drink.

"Hello, August." I smiled despite myself, peeking over at him after ordering a beer–the only one I saw on tap behind the bar. For some reason, I always found August's grumpiness to be somewhat...endearing. It was predictable, and I liked things that were predictable. "You can thank Mark for pointing me your way."

August grunted before taking a sip of his beer.

"So you're staying at the Evergreen Inn?" he asked, surprising me with the conversational turn of that question. I'd expected him to ignore me after his initial greeting. If it could even be considered a greeting.

"No," I said, followed by a self-deprecating laugh. "I'm staying at the Emerald Inn."

That got August's attention. His head turned just slightly, his eyes swiveling in my direction. And there it was–that molten hot gaze that turned my insides to mush. His eyes flashed with awareness as they connected with mine, almost like he felt the same jolt of heat inside him as I did. But that couldn't be.

My biggest predicament in this situation was honestly not that I'd had to take two planes, a bus, and a ferry to get to Evergreen Isle. It wasn't even that I was currently stranded without a place to stay. It was the fact that every time my boss insisted I interview August, I internally panicked.

To say I suffered from undeniable physical attraction to August Fletcher was a gross underestimation. And every time I talked to him, I felt like I was two seconds away from saying–or, God forbid, doing–something that would seriously risk my job. The job I very much needed if I wanted to continue living in my overpriced, undersized NYC apartment.

And now I was supposed to spend my summer trailing August around a beachy island to write a flashy retirement piece on him. I wasn't concerned about getting the story done, but I was worried about the secret agenda the team gave me: convince him to come back to New York and out of retirement.

August didn't exactly seem like the kind of guy who took advice from team beat writers.

In other words, from the heat in his gaze to the unwillingness of his attitude, I'd been set up with an impossible assignment.

"The Emerald Inn is on Emerald Isle," he said dryly as he traced his thumb around the rim of his glass like a soft caress. It distracted me, my eyes following the circular motion until his thumb picked up a droplet of beer, and he lifted his hand to suck it into his mouth, cleaning it off.

I gulped and forced my thoughts back to what he'd said, which in turn made me want to roll my eyes.

I couldn't even make a thank you, captain obvious comment because I was the one who'd missed that in the first place.

"It would seem I...made a booking error."

August's light brown eyes flicked over me, causing the familiar prickle of goosebumps to spread from head to toe. I was reasonably certain that he didn't realize what he was doing when he looked at me like that. August always struck me as one of those guys who didn't know the effect they had on people.

And then, something miraculous happened.

August's lip twitched in the faintest, tiniest version of a smile. But it was more than I'd ever noticed before.

"So what's your plan, Miss Castle?" he asked.

Was he amused? That I was stranded?

"Don't have a plan yet," I said tightly. And don't call me miss. It comes across mockingly."

He raised a brow—as if to say that was the point. I knew he'd be somewhat of an ass about me being here.

"You always have a plan," he said after a pause, running the pad of his thumb over the glass's rim again.

"You say that like you know me."

He pursed his lips before looking back at his nearly empty beer. He drained the rest in one gulp, pushing the glass to the side. "It doesn't seem fair, does it?"

"What?"

"That you always get to ask me question after question, and I never get to ask one back."

"That's kind of how interviews work, August."

His lips twitched again. It must be the island air, getting him to loosen up. But before I had too much time to contemplate it, August slid off his barstool and jerked his head toward the back of the bar.

"C'mon, Castle."

He didn't wait for me to respond before sauntering away, and I tried not to admire how good he could make a simple, white tee look. Thick muscles rippled over his back, tensing and flexing as he walked. That was probably what did the trick, although maybe it was the hot confidence. I hated how certain he seemed that I'd follow him across the bar without a second thought.

But then again, I'd traveled across states just to talk to him, and my job depended on it. It wasn't like I had a ton of other options—and he knew it.

"What are you doing?" I called after him, trailing my suitcase as I tried to catch up.

"I'm playing pool," he said, grabbing a cue and thrusting it in my face. "And you're playing with me. Every game you win, you get to ask me a question. Every game I win, I get to ask you a question."

With that explanation taken care of, August started racking the balls with lazy precision.

I cleared my throat. "That will take forever, and I have to figure out where I'm staying tonight. Unless you have a boat to get me to Emerald Isle."

"No boat," August replied without looking up. "But I have something even better."

"Oh, yeah?" I leaned forward onto the edge of the pool table. "And what's that?"

Finally giving me his full attention, August mimicked my pose, sliding his elbows over the table's surface as he bent over the racked balls. He leaned forward until we were at eye level, and his husky voice dropped a degree when he spoke.

"I have a bed."

I choked down a surprised cough, ignoring the burning in my chest–and other areas–from his words.

"I'm not going to sleep in your bed, August," I said flatly, meeting his smokey gaze. But even as I said the words, my pulse tripled as if protesting my protest. God, my traitorous heart rate needed to get the picture that ideas like that had no business being here. I had a job to do, and it did not include sleeping with August Fletcher.

A slow smirk slid onto August's face. "You make it sound like such an awful option."

Sleeping in a bed with August with his muscled, hard form pressed up against me did not sound like an awful option. But it did sound like a great way to get fired.

I felt August's low chuckle reverberate, getting under my skin. 'I didn't mean my bed, Castle. Believe it or not, I have more than one bed at my house."

Oh, right. Of course. That made a lot more sense. After living in a studio apartment for the last few years, I forgot that some people actually had more than one bedroom in their homes.

"I'm not going to stay with you," I insisted. But even as I attempted to protest, my body leaned further over the pool table, unable to resist the pull of August. Staying with him would be a terrible idea. I should at least try to find another option.

August shrugged, but I didn't miss the way his jaw clenched. He pushed off the table without saying anything else, so I took it to mean...suit yourself.

"Do you want to break?" he asked, nodding toward the table.

"I don't really know how."

"I'll teach you." He stepped back and gestured for me to line up in front of the rack of balls.

Indulging August in this game of pool was the last thing I should be doing. But I couldn't pass it up if it allowed me to ask some of my burning questions.

"Football, pool...what other things are you a pro at?" I teased as I took my place beside the table. Maybe he'd retired because he had other sports prospects that I didn't know about.

I felt August's body press closer from behind, his gravelly voice washing over me. "You haven't earned your question yet, Castle."

Damn him.

"Can you just show me how to do this already?" I laughed before my breath hitched embarrassingly when he touched me.

August's rough hands slid past my wrists, maneuvering my fingers to hold the cue properly. And then—to my slight horror—his large body covered mine as he bent me over the pool table. The feeling of his hips pressing closer to my ass caused me to quickly realize what an awful mistake this was.

Ten minutes. I only made it ten minutes before falling into a toe-curling trap.

Not that I thought August meant for it to be a trap. He was just doing anything he could so he wouldn't have to answer questions.

But if he kept this up all summer?

"Loosen up, Castle," August directed, wrapping his body around mine like he could get my limbs to melt. Which, well, he could. "What, have you never been bent over a pool table before?"

Fuck, I didn't know if I would make it.

Especially not without losing my job.

"As a matter of fact, I haven't," I said hotly. "Maybe someday someone will do me the honors of doing it properly."

With a low grunt, August's grip tightened around me.

And I immediately knew that had been the wrong thing to say.

a/n:

Hmm I get the feeling august would really like to do the honors of showing Quinn how it's done, what do you think?

Thanks so much for reading! let me know your thoughts on chapter one! □

xoxo amelie

two | a game for two

"THOSE BARS IN New York too uppity for anyone to show you how it's done on a pool table, huh?"

My head spun, trying to comprehend what August was saying while simultaneously digesting the way his fingers skimmed over my skin. If he noticed my goosebumps, he didn't say anything.

Which was good since I still hadn't recovered from the other thing that had come out of his mouth. I wasn't sure if he was talking about breaking the rack of balls or having sex on a pool table, but it didn't really matter, seeing as I didn't have experience with either.

"You haven't earned your question yet, Fletcher," I said, shooting his words back at him.

I felt a low rumble vibrate from his chest, shaking my ribcage. He was so close and all-encompassing as he reached around me that I could feel everything.

"Then let's get this game started," August murmured before showing me how to pull the cue back. He released my wrists once I was in place, letting me strike the white ball on my own. I hit it dead on and with enough force that it flew into the stack of solid and striped balls, dispersing them across the table.

But nothing fell into a pocket, and I stepped back in disappointment.

This was going to take a long time, and I was eager to get to work.

"I propose a change of rules." I leaned against the table, facing August. He assessed me with one raised brow, waiting for me to continue. "Every ball in the pocket earns a question," I said. "I'm not waiting until the end of the game to make conversation."

August's expression remained flat, seemingly unimpressed with my suggestion. But then again, August always seemed unimpressed. When the Warriors won the Super Bowl two seasons ago, August barely cracked a grin.

"Or we could just, I don't know..." He sighed heavily. "Drink a beer, listen to the music, and play some pool."

"You don't even have a drink."

"Well, that's easily solved." Without breaking eye contact, August hollered behind him. "Hey, Sunny! What about another Islander?"

"On it, Auggie," the man behind the bar shouted back. Sunny himself, presumably.

August's expression remained steady as if daring me to argue with his logic now. So I said, "There's also not any music playing."

August chuckled slightly before tipping his head at something behind me. I spun to see a jukebox in the corner, tucked away like someone hoped no one would notice it if they put it there.

"So what do you want to listen to, Castle?" August asked, exasperation evident as he walked around the table to the jukebox.

"The music was your suggestion," I pointed out. "I thought it would be better to have a chance to talk. You know, maybe about why you abruptly retired from the National Football League when you were at the top of your–"

August cut me off with a blast of a country tune I didn't recognize. Then he sauntered to the bar to grab the beer Sunny had produced. He swiped it off the counter before meeting my stare.

I should have known this entire assignment would be impossible. Usually, I liked interviews because they were repetitive, a conversation that was scripted. I knew my lines and what I needed to say to get others to respond how I wanted.

But it never worked like that with August.

He didn't play by the book, meaning everything between us felt like improv.

It was different.

Refreshing, in a way.

"There," he challenged, adjusting the music so it wasn't so loud. "Happy, now?"

But also infuriating.

I pretended to consider my answer for approximately half a second. "Not really, actually. Either we play a question per ball, or you can play pool with yourself, Fletcher."

If he wanted to make this into a little game, then fine. I'd play, but we were doing it my way.

August crossed the nearly-dead bar, eyes pinned on me. "Are you sure that's really what you want?"

He said it with a devastatingly low voice that sparked a bit of warning. But I was never good at paying attention to those.

I stuck one hand on my hip. "Why not?"

"Fine," he said, throwing one hand up in a sign of defeat. "For every pocketed ball, a question."

"Really?" I couldn't help my smile of victory.

My mom would say I went into sports reporting because I loved to write and tell stories to the world. My dad would say it was because of my competitive nature. I'd consider both of them to be right.

"If that's what you want, Castle," August said, but I didn't miss how his eyes glimmered as he took his place beside the pool table.

"You know it's really weird that you keep repeating that," I said warily.

August just shrugged—his favorite deflection tactic—and flicked his cue into position with a move that both startled and impressed me. But not nearly as much as when he lined up the stick with the white ball, striking it with the exact precision needed to rocket a striped ball into a corner pocket.

"So," he drawled, not wasting any time as he spun around to face me. He sat on the table's edge, thighs straining against worn jeans as he twirled the cue between his legs, balancing with his pointer finger on the top. "How much money did they have to fork over to get you to come all the way out here?"

Goddamn him.

Not only was he already beating me at my version of the game, but he was also acting and looking devastatingly hot while doing it.

Great. Just great.

I took a long drink of the Islander lager before leveling him with a look.

"You might be surprised to hear this, but that's not how it works in a normal job. Reporters don't have agents who negotiate for them. And if your boss tells you to go to Evergreen Isle, then you go to Evergreen Isle."

August nodded, unbothered by my sarcasm. "So how did–"

"Ah," I cut him off. "If that's another question, it's gonna have to wait, Fletcher."

Lips pressed together, August used the cue stick to push himself back to his feet. He leaned over the table with slow precision, and I didn't know if he was doing it to mock me or give me a show, but I could hardly complain when his back muscles flexed like that while getting the cue into place.

A second later, August sank another striped ball in a pocket. He whipped back around to face me, trying–and failing–to keep the smug expression off his face.

"So, how did Parker take that?"

"Parker?" I repeated. "How did Parker take me coming down here?"

August nodded, eyes burning into mine.

My coworker, Finn Parker, couldn't give less of a shit that I was here–as long as it was me instead of him. In fact, everyone back at the office was glad they weren't in my shoes.

"He doesn't care," I said, only that made August's brows draw inward. "You aren't his biggest fan, so...."

So why the hell would August think Finn would want to come down here and spend time with a guy who hates him?

"No," August grumbled, crossing his arms over his chest. "I'm definitely not."

I cocked my head to the side. "And why is that?"

The corner of his lips twitched. "Ah, is that a question you're trying to sneak by me?"

"Well, it would be helpful if you missed a ball, so I could have a chance," I muttered.

"This is how you wanted to play, Castle," August said matter-of-factly before shoving a hand in his pocket and returning to the table to survey it for his next move.

A move that unsurprisingly sank another ball.

"Do you have any pets?" he asked, this time from across the table. Both hands braced the edge as he pinned me with a look that seemed far too severe considering the question.

"Yes."

"What kinds are–"

"Another ball, Fletcher."

He sank it within less than a minute, and I sighed heavily.

"I have a hedgehog named Eloise."

"Is Parker watching Eloise?"

"My parents are watching her," I answered before biting down on my tongue when I realized I'd let information slip for free. "What's with all the Parker questions?"

"That's a question you haven't earned," he tsked.

"I just answered one of yours for free."

"That's your slip-up, not mine."

I glared at him, and he stared back. Eventually, he lifted a shoulder, giving in.

"Frankly, I was concerned for Eloise. Plus, I think you're wrong."

"What?"

"That inept man follows you around like a lovesick puppy," August grunted, sweeping his eyes down to look at our physical playing field and ignoring our mental one. "What's he gonna do with himself now that you're not in New York?"

"Love-sick?" I laughed, trying to conceal the way my stomach flipped. "It's not like that with Parker. I'm barely even friends with him."

August's head jerked back up to look at me, his eyes flashing as they settled on me. They blazed in a way that affected my internal body temperature, spearing me with heat. His lips slowly pursed in thought.

"Barely friends, huh?" he finally said. "You guys talk a lot for being barely friends."

"We're coworkers," I said flatly, ignoring how it made me feel when August gave me so much of his intense attention. "Also, I talk to a lot of people at work. Talking to people is kinda my job."

"Yeah..." August grumbled, his eyes falling off me, letting me breathe again. "I don't know why you signed up for that gig."

I shrugged. "You signed up to pummel people into the ground, and I'm not judging you."

One side of his mouth slipped upward in a crooked smile. "It's because you know it sounds fun."

"It wouldn't be my first choice."

"Hm," August hummed, eyes wandering back to my face before returning to the pool game at hand. He paced the outer ring of the table before finally settling on an angle to attack the ball.

Another striped one down, in the pocket.

He took his time sipping his beer before settling on a question.

"Why the Warriors?"

"Because I like New York."

He wrinkled his nose, making his feelings on the subject perfectly clear.

And because I felt the need to defend my statement, I added, "It's what I know, Fletcher. It's familiar, it's comforting, it's become my home."

"And it's only comforting because it's familiar," he argued. "You want to talk about comfort? Take a look around, Castle."

I did as he demanded, taking stock of the run-down bar with a few beer-hugging patrons sitting at wobbly wooden tables. Yes, there was a pleasant, beachy feel to the white shuttered windows and floor coated in dust and sand, but it didn't scream comfort. At least not for me.

"I'm not sure what you're trying to prove here, Auggie," I said, emphasizing the nickname the bartender gave him.

"Hey, now. Watch your tongue when you're talkin' about Sunny's." His jaw set as he jerked his head toward the bar. "Do you see that man behind the counter?"

"Let me guess, that's Sunny," I drawled.

"Yep," he said with a pride that was sort of endearing. "Uncle Sunny."

"Your family owns this?" I asked, and when he nodded, I continued. "See? This is home for you, like New York is to me. You're only comfortable here because it's familiar. It's not any different."

August took a long sip of his beer. Brown eyes watched me over the curve of the glass as he swallowed, licking his lips in a way that had me wondering what they felt like. If I had to guess, kissing August would be rough and demanding... and hot. Oh, so hot. Like the way he was looking at me.

He took a few steps forward, crowding my body against the pool table. Once again, we were close enough that my pulse began to race, taking off without a care for my heart health.

His voice slid in a silky caress across my skin. "I guess I'll just have to show you everything that Evergreen has to offer."

I mimicked him, draining the rest of my glass before lowering my voice to reply.

"I guess you will."

|||

By the time August was leading me out of the bar, I had to hold onto my suitcase for dear life in hopes of staying upright. By some grace of God, I made it to his car—but even in my drunken state, I recognized how much of a struggle it was to get there.

And August?

Oh, he was mad.

Pissed as all hell.

I couldn't help but find it amusing. I'd been giggling like a schoolgirl with no hope of stopping, and that only infuriated August more. Which only made me laugh more.

He'd stopped drinking a long time ago. Hours, maybe? I wasn't even sure how many games of pool he beat me in or how many things I'd said that I likely shouldn't have. Because I, foolishly, had not set aside my beer until the very end...not until it was too late.

"You should have told me you didn't eat dinner, Quinn," he scolded through clenched teeth as he watched to make sure I buckled myself into his car.

I ignored the tone of his voice and focused instead on how he did, actually, know my first name. I'd been starting to wonder.

"Eat," he demanded, pointing at the three boxes of fried food sitting in my lap that he'd asked Uncle Sunny to make for me even though the kitchen had closed over an hour ago.

"You have a car," I commented, opening the top box to munch on a pile of fries.

"Of course I have a car," August grunted as he jammed the key into the ignition.

I shrugged. "This just seems like the kind of place where everyone rides their bicycles around to eliminate carbon emissions or something."

August snorted. "Not that kind of island. Try over at Emerald Isle."

"I'll let you know when I check into my hotel tomorrow."

"You're not going to stay there." His words were as tight as his body while he maneuvered the car onto the street. "You're going to stay with me, finish your little story, and then get out of my hair. You'll be returning to your precious New York before you know it. Eloise will be thrilled."

I froze, french fry halfway to my mouth as panic worked through my veins. August was in for a rude awakening if he thought I'd be out of his hair that fast. If I showed my face back in New York before either getting some serious dirt on this football player or convincing him to return for the season, well...I could kiss my job goodbye.

"Your hospitality is astounding, Fletcher," I said with as much sweetness as I could muster. I wasn't sure it was effective between the slurring of my words.

His eyes flicked over to me and then landed on the french fry. When I popped it into my mouth, he grunted in satisfaction.

"Not exactly something I'm known for," he said, gaze swiveling back to the dark road. "You shouldn't be surprised."

"I'm not," I snorted before dissolving into a giggle fit again.

He sighed. "Like I said, you'll only have to deal with me for a little bit."

August's hands gripped the steering wheel tighter, focused on driving us off toward a dark, remote corner of the island. I cursed myself again for fucking up my hotel reservations. And then once more when August turned to look at me, a smirk sliding onto his ruggedly handsome face.

If I was sober, maybe I'd have the energy to stop this entire situation from happening. But as it was, I'd just have to trust August Fletcher.

"Maybe you'll find out I'm not so bad after all, Castle," he murmured.

Fuck. I trusted August to keep me safe tonight, but I absolutely did not trust him to keep my job safe.

Because if only August knew...finding out that he wasn't so bad was precisely what I was afraid of happening.

a/n:

thank you so much to everyone who picked up this new book and gave it a try! I appreciate you all sm □ thoughts on chapter two?

xoxo amelie

three | no more games

M Y PILLOW WAS as hard as a rock.

It was also hot to the touch, and I couldn't flip it over to get the cold side.

In fact, I had a feeling that it didn't have a cold side. I had a feeling that both sides were hot and hard, so very, very hot and hard.

Because my pillow was a man. And if my fuzzy memory was any help, he wasn't just any man.

He was August Fletcher.

Which meant—oh shit.

A weird strangled noise flew from my lips as I rolled over, away from my makeshift pillow in the shape of the NFL's biggest star. The same one who held my career in the palm of his hands.

His very large, capable hands which had just swooped in around my waist, hoisting me back into the bed.

I cried out in protest, hoping that some of the noises leaving my mouth were words, but I couldn't be sure. To my own ears, I sounded garbled and water-logged. And it felt like something was growing on my tongue.

"Relax, Castle." August's rough voice had an odd, soothing effect. and my body immediately did as he commanded. "You were about to fall off the goddamn bed and straight into your puke bucket."

Puke bucket?

Oh my God.

No wonder my mouth tasted like shit.

His hand vanished a moment later after I'd been deposited next to him again. I looked up at his handsome face through blurry vision, and reality came crashing down as the sun blinded me, streaming in through the windows.

"I'm in your bed," I breathed.

"You're in my bed," he agreed.

Even though I had said it, and he had said it, my brain was still struggling to put the pieces together.

"You said you had more than one bed," I said.

I didn't remember everything from last night, but I sure as hell remembered that.

"I do have more than one bed," he said, nodding. Those smokey eyes studied me, shining with slight amusement as I slid the covers higher over my body. Maybe if I could just disappear, we could forget that this happened.

"And, what, you just didn't want to get the sheets dirty on the other one?"

His eyes rolled up. "You needed supervising."

"Look, I know I'm younger than you, but I'm not a child."

He leaned back against the headboard, assessing me. "I'm well aware you're not a child. But you were a very drunk twenty-six-year-old last night."

I stared at him. "How do you know my age?"

He shrugged. "I'll bet you know mine."

"It's my job to know things about you, Fletcher."

His birthday was in October. He didn't like celebrating it. And this year, he'd be turning thirty-seven.

"That sounds like a boring job," August said dryly. Then he folded two broad, muscled arms across his chest. His bare chest. God, he was tan. All bronze and shimmering. My eyes followed the trail of muscles down to where a blanket covered his waist, and oh my God–

My eyes darted back to his face. "Please tell me you're wearing pants."

He lifted a brow without responding. His expression said...why don't you find out?

But I'd been baited by this man all last night to say and do things I likely shouldn't have. And while I took full responsibility for drinking too much and playing his little pool game for far too long, I refused to continue making poor decisions.

"I'm wearing pants," August sighed, giving in. He threw the blanket off his lap, and I realized that not only was he wearing sweatpants, but he was also sitting on top of the covers that I was beneath on the bed. His blanket had been completely separate. "You will find that you, also, are wearing pants."

I wiggled my legs beneath the covers and knew he was telling the truth. By the feel of it, I was wearing the same pair of worn jeans as yesterday, and man, was I suddenly feeling uncomfortable and trapped in them.

"You didn't think to tell the drunk girl to change into her pajamas?"

"I figured suggesting that the drunk girl take off her clothes would be considered ungentlemanly."

The expression he gave me was stoic and serious, and I couldn't help but laugh outright at it. "Okay, Fletcher. I appreciate you protecting my honor. But if we ever find ourselves in this situation again—"

"God, I hope not."

"—I'm giving you consent right now to make me put on some comfortable clothes."

"Noted, but there's no way I'm gonna let you get that drunk again," he grunted before pushing off the bed, standing.

Damn, I forgot how tall he was. And just...big. Average men did not fill up a room like that.

I kicked my covers off with a yawn, feeling surprisingly well-rested. My head definitely felt a bit foggy and heavy, like it was filled with all the sand from the beach. But beyond that, I couldn't complain. Likely because I'd already emptied my stomach of everything I ate and drank yesterday. Emphasis on drank.

August rounded the bed, keeping his eyes on his feet. "I put your bags by the bathroom." He pointed to the side of the room without lifting his head. "Feel free to freshen up. You know, take your pants off. I'll be making breakfast."

Without another word—or even glance—my way, he was gone.

I blew a breath from my lips and looked around the room for the first time.

Simply put, it was beautiful. Decorated in hues of navy and white with natural wood trim lining the floors and doorways, it had an earthy, beachy feel. I wondered if August had hired an interior decorator. I couldn't imagine him at a store, picking out throw pillows to compliment his bedspread. And yet, everything matched perfectly.

When I walked into the bathroom, I gasped.

If the bedroom was nice, the bathroom was marvelous.

All the cabinetry was done in that same natural wood, giving the room warmth. Then the black casing of the shower and the hardware used throughout took that warmth and turned it up a notch. The lighting was moody as I flicked the switch by the door, and sensuality oozed from the space. The musky smell of man filled my senses.

Using August's bathroom suddenly felt way more intimate than sleeping in his bed.

Trying to put all those thoughts out of my mind, I hurried to freshen up as August had so lovingly put it. And, to his credit, I did look like a mess. Embarrassment burned brighter within me, but I pushed it down as I strode out of his room in a simple white sundress.

Unsurprisingly, the rest of August's house was equally as stunning. He must have had it built or remodeled recently because everything was on trend.

It was a bit odd because August was the type of person who tended to go against the mold. But I couldn't blame him for wanting to have a nice house. He'd certainly worked hard for it over the years.

"Here," he grunted, pushing forward a plate piled with eggs, bacon, and toast. "I've gotta make sure you eat today."

I resisted the urge to roll my eyes. "I don't usually forget, you know. It was just a busy day of travel, and when I finally found you, I didn't want to waste any time."

August didn't say anything in response, but his lips dipped further into a frown.

Great.

"Thank you, by the way." My voice sounded hoarse, so I cleared it before continuing. "For letting me stay last night and making sure I didn't choke on my own vomit. And breakfast looks great."

"Considering the entire Warriors organization likely knows you're here, it would not have ended well for me if you choked on your own vomit. Everyone would know exactly where to look when you didn't return to New York."

"Once again, your hospitality is appreciated."

I said it teasingly, matching his tone. But I meant it.

To say that August Fletcher was antisocial was an understatement. I was more than aware that he likely hated having guests. I knew he didn't enjoy interviews. And even though he never agreed to let anyone interview him but me, I'd still expected him to shut me out, walk away, and leave me high and dry when he saw me in his hometown bar.

So while it was clear he wasn't exactly happy that a Warriors reporter sat across from him at his kitchen countertop, he hadn't kicked me out yet.

And that, honestly, was a miracle.

His heavy sigh interrupted my thoughts.

"Let's get this over with."

I raised a brow while biting into a strip of crispy bacon.

He wanted to...talk?

"No more games this morning, Fletcher? You're not going to make me beat you in darts or something this time?"

"I don't think you could beat me in darts." He put his hands on his hips and surveyed the rest of the bacon sizzling in the pan. Thankfully he'd put on a shirt, making it a little bit easier for me to think straight. But then he looked up at me, eyes piercing mine, and my thoughts started running in circles again. "So what do you want to know, Castle?"

I sat up straighter. Was he really going to make it that easy for me?

"Why did you retire so abruptly?"

He pursed his lips. "Next question."

"That's a pretty big question to skip."

"Maybe I don't want to answer it."

I shrugged. "I can't make you."

But I also wouldn't be leaving until I learned something about it.

"What else do you want to know?"

"Well..." I shifted nervously in my chair. "I'm here to experience your life in retirement."

"Experience it?" he repeated, mulling the words over.

"I want to know...well, everything. What you're doing with your newfound freedom, if you have any other pursuits, if you've developed new business ventures or hobbies."

"There's not much to tell."

"Everyone thought you might say that. Which is why I'm here to see for myself."

"Meaning..."

"Meaning I'm not going anywhere anytime soon, Fletcher." I sipped the orange juice he put in front of me. It tasted fresh. "But I'll find another place to stay and get out of your hair–"

"That seems contradictory," he said, cutting off my impersonation of his words from last night. I remembered just enough of our car ride home to recall him saying that. "For you to find somewhere else to stay when you're supposed to...experience my life."

He said the last words like he thought they were ridiculous. He made a little scoffing sound in the back of his throat, which I chose to ignore.

"Look, I'm not trying to be a nuisance. I'm just trying to do my job."

"You'll stay here," he said with a note of finality. "In the guest room, of course. And I'll help you do your job."

I stared at him. On one hand, staying here would blur our professional boundaries even more. And I needed to keep those intact. But on the other hand, living with August would give me the most unfiltered access to his life for my piece.

I couldn't pass that up.

"Excellent." I smiled, hoping I might coax one out of him too. I'd caught a glimpse of one a few times last night, so I knew it was possible. "What's first on the agenda of a day in the life of August Fletcher?"

He cocked his head to the side, considering me.

"What?" I wiped at my mouth, hoping I didn't have something on my face. Considering the state he saw me in last night, I didn't need to make a fool of myself again.

But then August asked a question I definitely hadn't been expecting.

"Did you pack a swimsuit?"

a/n:

Quinn: I really gotta to be more professional hereAugust: sooo bikini?

thanks for reading!! xoxo amelie

four | getting burnt

THE WARRIORS HAD KNOWN what they were doing, sending Quinn Castle to my doorstep. Or bar, rather.

Not only was she the one reporter I didn't hate on staff, but she was also impossible to turn away. If Parker had shown up here, I would have had no problem leaving him high and dry to find his own place to stay. I would have had no problem telling Parker, or another of the other reporters, to fuck off.

But Quinn Castle?

She was too innocent.

I was pretty sure she had no idea what her boss had done to me, and I was also pretty sure she had no idea what it did to my dick every time she laughed.

God, this was a fucking nightmare. I came back to Evergreen Isle to try to recollect myself, to find a bit of peace in my life again. But I wasn't going to have any peace while Quinn was here.

Part of it was my fault.

Did I have to insist she stay with me?

No, of course not.

Did I have to ask if she packed a swimsuit?

Definitely not.

Did I have to put her in my bed last night?

Debatable.

It was either she slept in my bed or I slept in hers—just so I could keep an eye on her cute, but drunk, ass. Even if it was a bit torturous.

Actually, a bit was an understatement.

Fuck.

I clearly wasn't thinking with my head right now.

Hearing the door slide open behind me, I twisted to face the house and the woman coming out. I leaned against the side of my back deck, gripping the railing hard as I took in the sight of Quinn Castle in a goddamn bikini.

It was canary yellow, and it looked so fucking good against her lightly tanned skin. Hell, she glowed as she walked across the deck toward me with way too much pep in her step. Enough pep in her step that the tiny strips of fabric on her body were struggling to do their job.

And if that wasn't bad enough, Quinn walked straight past me to jump into the sand, and I nearly died on the spot when I realized her bikini bottoms weren't even close to covering her ass cheeks.

I should have known better than to invite even more torture into my life.

It had been torture enough sitting through countless interviews with Quinn over the last few seasons, and then she'd at least been fully clothed.

"Are you coming?" Quinn called over her shoulder, and I swallowed. Hard.

I was surprised she agreed to this arrangement. She'd always been careful around me, always carefully treading the line between professional discourse and flirting. We'd danced that dance on more than one occasion, mostly because I was such a fucking sucker for this woman's smile. The real one. Not the plastered, fake one she used at work.

If I could catch sight of it once or twice in an interview, I would consider it a success. And then I'd retreat, walk away, and wonder if she would ever be interested in talking to me if she wasn't paid to. Likely not. She was too young for me. Too happy and wholesome and pure.

Although, considering the way Quinn was swaying her hips, beckoning me to follow her, maybe I wasn't right about that last part. And there had been a dare in her eyes last night, even before she got drunk. Heat that had nothing to do with the summer sun.

She claimed to love New York, but I had a feeling the city and that godforsaken organization only subdued her. In contrast, island life looked good on her.

Really fucking good.

I adjusted my semi-hard cock in my swim shorts before stepping off the deck and into the hot sand. But I didn't get far before my phone buzzed in my hand. I peeked at it before walking further.

COHEN: see you fuckers tonight

FINNY: i'll be there

FINNY: wouldn't miss a chance to watch you both cry when I beat you for the third week in a row.

Shit, was it already Tuesday again?

I never missed pool nights with the guys, but the last thing I wanted to do was introduce Cohen and Finley to Quinn. And I had a feeling that until she left Evergreen Isle, she'd be on my ass everywhere I went.

ME: sorry boys, can't make it tonight.

I pocketed my phone before I could read their responses, which were bound to give me shit for bailing. I could come up with an excuse later. An excuse that had nothing to do with the hot Warriors reporter who was in town to write a retirement piece on me.

Fuck that.

The Warrior organization should know damn well what they did to piss me off and high tail it out of there as soon as I fucking could.

Quinn legitimately seemed to have no idea, though.

Quinn also seemed to have no idea what it was doing to me as she bent over to spread her towel onto the sand.

Jesus fuck, this woman.

Thank God this part of the island was scarcely occupied. I had a few neighbors along this part of the beachfront, but they were mostly wealthy folks who rarely visited their beach house. This morning, the sand and the surf were ours.

"I don't know why you're lying down," I called over to her as I grabbed my surfboard from under my deck and tucked it beneath my arm. Quinn's eyes widened as they flicked from my face to my board. "What?" I chuckled. "You asked what my day looks like, and I start it by surfing."

Quinn cocked her head to the side, watching as I walked over to her. "Don't you think soaking up the sun on the nice, dry land sounds much more enjoyable?"

"No."

My blood ran hot, meaning that if I didn't let the ocean cool me off soon, I wouldn't last another five minutes standing here in the sand. Standing next to Quinn.

Quinn laughed despite her obvious wariness. "Fine. I'll soak up the sun, and you can enjoy the waves."

"Hm." I raised a brow while glancing down at her. She was nearly a foot shorter than me, which meant my view from this angle was...distracting. I focused on her eyes instead, which glittered in the summer sun. "I thought you wanted the August Fletcher experience."

She crossed her arms over her chest, and man, did I wish she hadn't done that. "I think I can capture the experience from the shore just fine, thank you very much."

"C'mon, Castle." I shot her a smirk. "Get a little wet with me."

Quinn's caramel eyes grew even wider. Shit, I had to get my fucking mouth in check if I was going to survive this interview process. I had no right flirting with her now any more than I did when we were in New York, but it was so much harder to rein it in when we were out here with none of the usual hawks watching over us.

Plus, I loved watching the war inside her head as she tried to figure out how to respond. Meanwhile, a pretty flush dusted her skin, and I wondered how hot it would feel to the touch.

Finding out would likely burn us both.

"I think I'll just watch," she said, her voice breathy.

I shrugged. That was probably for the best. At least one of us was using common sense. As enjoyable as seeing Quinn up on a surfboard would be, it'd likely be more of a tease. And I didn't know how much more of that I could handle.

"You can just swim, then," I offered.

Quinn looked at the waves crashing against the shore. Suspicion danced in her eyes, almost like the water was about to commit a crime.

"No thanks," she said before plopping down on her towel. "I'll be right here."

I considered her for a second longer before taking off for the water. I could feel Quinn's eyes on my bare back as I walked, and I wondered what the hell was going on in that head of hers. I probably didn't want to know.

There were a few good swells this morning, but I spent more time sitting in the lineup than riding in the pocket of any waves. Honestly, I missed my shot at a few of them and decided that maybe I was just too distracted to enjoy it this morning.

How funny that Quinn was here because she wanted to know what my life was like after retirement, and her fucking presence messed with the reality of it.

I trudged back out of the ocean's spray, running a hand through my wet hair as I made my way to where Quinn sat in the sand. Her ever-watchful eyes trailed over me, but I'd be damned if that look she gave me was only for research purposes.

"You sure you don't want to give it a try?" I asked.

"I'm sure." She smiled before shifting on her towel.

The change in position brought her shoulders into my direct line of vision, and I internally cursed when I realized I hadn't even offered her some goddamn sunscreen this morning. Poor girl went from never seeing the light of day in her NYC office to being blasted with it, and her skin was not happy. Her slight summer city tan had nothing on the sun she'd get out here on the island.

"Christ, Castle." I sighed. "You're getting burnt to a goddamn crisp."

"Am I?" she gasped, tucking her chin to look at her chest, which was just as rosy as her shoulders. And then she tugged down her top a bit, giving me a fucking show as she evaluated the burn line on her skin. "Oh shit, you're right."

Averting my eyes, I dropped my board into the sand beside her. "I'll go get you some sunscreen."

"Thank you!" she called, but I was already halfway to the house and taking deep breaths to get my shit under control.

It was no use. No matter how many breaths I took on the way to the house, it couldn't calm me down enough to deal with the question Quinn asked me when I returned to the beach.

"Will you help me rub it in?" She asked it so innocently. I wasn't sure if I was fooled by it, but then she smiled at me, all breezy and unaffected. "Just my back where I can't reach."

Shit.

Quinn Castle was going to test all my goddamn willpower this summer.

And I had a feeling I was going to like it way too fucking much.

a/n:

at this point, they're just continually upping the ante on each other. hope you're here for that

thanks for reading! xoxo amelie

five | rubdowns

I STARED UP AT AUGUST while reclining on my beach towel after applying sunscreen to my front. It wasn't until I caught the way his jaw flexed that I realized how my question likely sounded.

Flirtatious. Teasing. Unprofessional.

That hadn't been my intention. Honestly. As much as August's hot body, handsome face, and surely-capable hands were hard to ignore, I hadn't been thinking with my vagina when I asked him to rub me down. I'd been more concerned with not looking even more like a roasted tomato in his golden, god-like presence.

"Turn over, Castle," August said gruffly. Three words, but my stomach made the tiniest flip at the sound of them. All his years of being an NFL team captain made his commands ooze confidence, and he had me turning over instantly.

I flipped onto my stomach, and August heaved a sigh. Of exasperation? I couldn't really tell. But it wasn't a happy sigh. It might have been an irritated sigh. Maybe because he realized his retirement had led him to this: rubbing sunscreen all over the Warriors reporter who had stalked him to his hometown.

"Do you want me to untie my straps?" I asked, turning my head to the side and resting it against the towel so I could still talk to him.

"Do I want you to untie your straps?" he repeated. "As in, take your top off?"

The last part came out choked, as though he couldn't believe I'd said that.

I couldn't believe I'd said that, either.

"Just thought it might make it easier," I mumbled.

The squirt of sunscreen hitting my back was so cold that I shivered. And then I shivered again when August's voice caressed my skin ahead of his hands. "If I find that I need to take your top off, I am perfectly capable of doing it."

I didn't doubt that for a minute. August likely had more than his fair share of experience with taking off women's tops. I'd documented a few of his flings over the years, although they never seemed to last long.

The thought sparked curiosity in me.

"So, August..."

"Here we go," he muttered under his breath, and I wasn't sure if he was referring to the line of questioning I was about to launch or the way his hands started smoothing the sunscreen across my back.

"Have you been seeing anyone lately?" I asked before clamping my mouth shut when August massaged the sunscreen into a pressure point, and a moan bubbled up from my throat.

"Christ, Castle," he grunted, his hands temporarily vanishing before they returned to spread sunscreen on my lower back.

"What?" My breath hitched as his fingertips dipped beneath the seam of my bikini bottoms, but then they moved into safer territory, and I somehow managed to recover. "I'm trying to get a scope of your life, including your dating habits, now that you've left the city."

"I wouldn't have offered for you to stay with me if I were seeing someone," he answered as he slicked his hands beneath my bikini straps and let them snap back into place against my skin. "I don't know many women who would be okay with that. Especially when you're...you."

I scrunched my brow. "What's that supposed to mean?"

He sighed one of those sighs again. "Nothing."

I wanted to push the question, but it wasn't what I should focus on. I couldn't write an article about how August felt about me; that was irrelevant. His dating life, on the other hand...

"Well, maybe you have something casual going on. Something non-exclusive?" I fished, switching back to our previous topic.

"I'm not that kind of guy," he muttered as he smoothed his hands back up to my neck, rubbing it in a way that made me want to close my eyes and let him massage me all over.

"You've dated casually," I pointed out, trying as hard as I could to focus on his words and not his touch.

There was a slight pause, and his hands stilled.

"I never considered any of those dates casual," he said bitterly. "But when I realized I was alone in thinking that, well...I'm sure you know."

Oh, shit.

"I'm sorry, August." I softened my tone. "I never really realized."

I'd thought he was just like most athletes we covered, enjoying the perks of his career and entertaining his flavor of the week. Because, in my mind, what woman wouldn't want a lasting relationship with a man like August Fletcher? Stable. Kind, although a little rough around the edges. Handsome, very handsome. Talented. A good income–to put it mildly.

When August didn't touch me again, I assumed he was done with the sunscreen application and turned over. I found him bent over me, blocking the sun with the outline of his broad shoulders. His face was tense, and I hated that I'd brought up something uncomfortable for him. I usually had better tact, but not being on new grounds clearly affected my judgment.

"People like to use me for temporary fame," he said with a shrug. "I'm used to it."

"Do you know what I would use you for?" I asked with a teasing smile.

August quirked a brow, his expression changing to something more lively and intrigued.

"Do I want to know?" he asked, his voice low enough that it made me wonder if this line of conversation was a good idea, considering my resolution to remain professional.

But then again, I'd just let August rub sunscreen all over me after sleeping in his bed last night, so maybe it was too late anyway.

"I would use you as a masseuse," I laughed. "Because the way you just put that sunscreen on my back was the best rubdown I'd had in a long time."

Okay, maybe those exact words hadn't been the right ones.

August's lips twitched in amusement, the curve of his mouth teasing me with how subtly hot it was. "The best rub down, huh? Suddenly I'm concerned about your dating life, Castle."

I gave him a playful shove, but he was immovable as he hovered over me. Of course he was.

"I didn't mean it like that."

Although my dating history wasn't exactly anything to brag about.

I grabbed the bottle of sunscreen from where he'd left it in the sand. "I'm not as skilled with my hands as you are, but I'd gladly return the favor if you want."

"Oh, yeah?" August chuckled. "You gonna give me a rub down?"

I rolled my eyes. "You have such a delightful sense of humor, Fletcher. Where has it been hiding all this time?"

"Here." August flopped back into the sand, digging his toes in and leaning back on his palms. "In Evergreen Isle."

He dipped his head back and closed his eyes, letting the sun hit his face. He really did seem remarkably at ease here. All of our interviews back in New York had seemed somewhat...pained. Like he couldn't wait to escape.

And now he had.

There had to be more, though. More to the reason he'd fled back here besides his love for his hometown.

"What else is here?" I asked, sitting into a position that mimicked his. "Besides your humor?"

His eyes flashed back open. He cocked his head to the side, considering my question.

"Uncle Sunny," he said.

"Who else?"

I knew he was an only child, and his parents had both passed. His dad in a car accident back when he was a teen, and his mom more recently. Although it was before I started working for the Warriors.

So, to my knowledge, August didn't have an immediate family living on Evergreen Isle. Did he come back just for his uncle? Or was there someone else?

"I have a few friends I've kept in touch with," he answered slowly.

"Any cousins?" I asked. "Does Sunny have kids?"

He nodded. "One of the friends is actually a cousin. We both pitch in at the bar when we can."

"Is that why you moved home?" I asked. "To help out?"

He shrugged before looking away, training his gaze down the coastline. "It was a factor."

"What were the other factors?"

August swiveled back around, and I felt a little electric shock when his eyes met mine again.

"You ask a lot of questions."

"We've been over this. It's kind of my job."

He considered that for a moment. "I just feel like I should get something in return."

"You got to ask all your questions last night."

"Something tells me your questions are going to last a lot longer than one night," he said with a little roll of his eyes.

"I already offered to rub sunscreen on your back." I shrugged, biting down on the ridiculous smile I was trying to keep off my face. I wasn't sure why, but I found his reluctance about this interview weirdly endearing. So many men loved to talk about themselves. All of my colleagues hated interviewing August because he was so hard to get answers out of. But I liked the challenge. The humble athletes were always my favorite. "I don't know what else you want from me."

August's eyes flicked over me before training back on the shoreline. "I'm sure I'll come up with something."

"As long as it doesn't involve me getting in the water," I said, hoping that wasn't where his thoughts were going.

He chuckled. "You're really not a fan of the ocean, are you, Castle?"

Not a fan was putting it lightly. There were far too many unknowns in the big, blue sea. And I'd watched one too many seasons of Shark Week.

"I'd prefer a nice lake over the ocean," I admitted, figuring that made it sound like a preference and less like an all-encompassing ridiculous fear.

"There aren't any lakes on Evergreen Isle."

I snapped my fingers together sarcastically. "Bummer."

August narrowed his eyes. "I'm starting to think you don't know how to swim."

"I know how to swim," I laughed. "I just prefer dry land." I tipped my head back, enjoying the sun like he did a few minutes ago. "This weather is nice."

"The heat's not as enjoyable when you're stuck in the city, is it?"

"No," I admitted, letting the hot day pulse over me. But I wasn't sure if the heat was from the sun or company. "It's not."

August stood, clearing his throat. "Personally, it's a bit too hot for me. I'm going to cool down in the water."

I watched him walk away, wondering, not for the first time, what I'd gotten myself into. And then I continued to wonder it for most of the morning, watching as August dashed in and out of the water every time he got just a little bit too warm.

And I especially wondered it when he eventually came out of the water for the last time, shook his hair out like a dog–a sexy dog, granted–and announced, "Let's go hop in the shower, Castle."

When I stared at him, unable to find words, he chuckled.

"Don't look at me like that. I have two showers just like I have two beds."

Right. Of course not together.

But...

"Forgive me for being alarmed, but I did end up in your bed last night despite your promise of me getting my own."

"We've been over this. You required supervision." He gave me a look that made my knees buckle as I attempted to stand. "Do you require supervision in the shower, Castle?"

"No," I replied breathlessly. "I don't."

But I soon learned that I was wrong about that, too.

a/n:

who are you when you go to the beach? Lounging in the sand, dry-land only like Quinn? Or a water-adventurer like August?

thanks for reading! hope you're enjoying so far □xoxo amelie

six | taking measurements

AUGUST'S SHOWER IN HIS guest bedroom was just as to-die-for as the one in the main suite. Natural wood combined with soft blue and white tiles made it feel like the island was alive right here in this bathroom. If I could live in this shower, I would; that was how much I loved it.

There were not one but two shower heads—a feature I loved until I turned them both on simultaneously, and they sprayed ice-cold water on me, causing me to let loose a high-pitched shriek of surprise.

Shivering, I jumped back out of the shower and tried to reach in to adjust the temperature. But before I could figure it out, a loud bang on the door made me jump, slipping back into the shower as I shrieked again. Luckily I was able to catch myself before I toppled over and wound up on the floor.

"Castle!" August's rough voice echoed in the bathroom, even through the door. "What's going on?"

"Nothing!" I called before sputtering when I got a mouth full of ice-cold water. Squeezing my eyes shut to shield them, I reached blindly for the shower dials but ended up groping the air instead. "Just—ugh. How do you—"

"I'm coming in," he announced.

I didn't have time to protest before August burst into the bathroom, and all I could think was how relieved I was to still be in my swimsuit. But all that relief vanished when I wiped the water out of my eyes and looked over to see a jaw-dropping sight.

August Fletcher wearing nothing but a towel draped around his waist.

August Fletcher wearing nothing but a towel, draped around his waist with rivulets of water running down his broad, glistening chest.

"Are you okay?" he croaked. He'd marched across the bathroom and now had one hand on either side of the shower door, sweeping his gaze over me as though searching for the problem. The first pass of his eyes was frantic and assessing. And then the second, once he realized there was no bodily harm, was slower and downright appreciative.

His gaze was the only bit of heat in this bathroom.

I wrapped my arms around myself as another shiver wracked through me. But I couldn't say for certain what caused it.

"You sank a lot of money into this beach house for it not to have hot water, Fletcher."

"Jesus, Castle." He hung his head momentarily. "You screamed bloody murder and scared the shit out of me."

"It startled me," I said defensively. "It's freezing."

Fumbling with the temperature dial again, I bounced on my tiptoes to stay warm as the cold water continued to rain down around me. August was blocking my way out of the shower, and I didn't dare step closer to him when I was half-naked and he was almost entirely naked.

August did not hold the same reservation. He stepped into the shower, crowding me against the wall as he batted my hand away, spinning the dial the opposite way. Then instead of getting out of the shower, he turned toward me while letting the water drench the towel around his waist.

I was determined not to look at that towel. Not right now. Not when I was entirely certain if I looked down, I'd see outlines of something I definitely should not be looking at.

So I looked up at August's face instead.

That was also a mistake. Water clung to his eyelashes as he blinked, his deep brown eyes sucking me in. I was so distracted that when he put his hands on each of my arms, I jolted in surprise. August's lips curved in amusement as he rubbed my arms up and down in what I could only assume was an attempt to warm me up until the water found the right temperature, which it was doing very slowly.

"I thought you didn't need supervision," he murmured.

I rolled my eyes but my mind was too distracted by his close proximity to reply.

"You're getting wet," I noted when I realized I needed to say something but couldn't figure out what.

"You're so perceptive." He cocked his head to the side, keeping his attention focused on me. "It's no wonder you became a reporter."

I swatted at his chest before immediately regretting it when my hand was met with a solid wall of muscle.

"You didn't need to come in here," I continued. "I would have figured it out."

"You would have," he agreed. "But I should have been a better host and explained it first."

"Do you get into the showers with all your guests, Fletcher? Or am I just special?"

I found myself hoping I was special. From watching his interactions with people during the Warriors season, I knew this version of August differed from the one most people saw. But maybe it was just the island air that made him like this. Maybe it was the comfort of his hometown and of-floading the stress of his career.

He laughed. "I'll let you figure that one out."

"You're no fun," I pouted.

August's lips fell flat, and his hands fell back to his sides. "That's what people tell me."

I immediately hated myself for saying that when it clearly hit a sore spot for August. Because the reality was that I had only been on Evergreen Isle for less than twenty-four hours, and I was already having more fun than I imagined I would when I'd been given this assignment. Some would argue that I was having too much fun.

"People don't know what they're talking about," I said, trying to sound reassuring.

August shrugged before tipping his head back and closing his eyes like he did on the beach early when he was soaking up the sun. Now, he was letting the warm water wash over him and running his hands through his hair to slick it back from his face. A nearly inaudible moan of appreciation slipped out of him, and that moan sent a shot of awareness through me.

I was sharing a shower with August Fletcher. Sure, he might be using a different showerhead than me, but we were in the same tiled rectangle, and steam was starting to swirl around us.

And because I was already in heaps of trouble where he was concerned, I took advantage of him having his eyes closed to slowly peruse how ridiculously gorgeous he looked when he was this close to me. Without his shirt on. With water running down his well-defined abs to the wet towel tied around his waist. The towel that was sticking to his hips and legs like a second skin, and–

"Trying to take my measurements, Castle?"

August's voice sounded thicker, more gravel-filled than the last he spoke.

I sputtered, lifting my guilty gaze back to his face. He smirked at me.

Goddamnit.

I cleared my throat. "Like you said, I'm very perceptive. I never know what I'm going to need to report on."

My voice came out scratchy, and I hoped it didn't give me away too much.

"Well," August murmured, his eyes sparkling between the water spray as he studied my face. "Before you go documenting too much, I'd like the record to show that I'm a grower...not a show-er."

It took me a second to understand what he was saying, and I felt my eyes grow round as the realization hit me.

"The record actually will not show any such thing, Fletcher," I huffed, reaching for the shampoo bottle I'd put in the corner before starting the shower. August clearly wasn't planning on leaving any time soon, so I might as well take advantage of the hot water while it lasted.

He lifted a brow. "You're going to do me dirty like that, Castle?"

"Oh, don't you worry. I'm just striking your dick size from the record completely. One, because I wasn't even looking at it. Please. And two, because I don't want to get fired."

August's lips pressed together, but they twitched as though he was trying not to laugh. I took a small step toward him, just enough that I was far enough out of the shower's spray to scrub shampoo into my hair, and August watched with amusement.

"Okay, Castle," he finally said before brushing his thumb across my temple, flicking suds off my now-scorching hot skin. "You're missing your hair completely and getting shampoo everywhere it's not supposed to be."

His eyes dropped momentarily, for a split second, to my chest before returning to my face.

"I'm sorry my shampoo technique isn't up to your standard," I said. "I'm not used to having anyone in my showers to judge me."

He bit down on his bottom lip, scraping it with his teeth as he contemplated my words. "That so?"

If I wasn't hot from the water, the steam rising around us, or August's toned muscles, I was definitely hot now. My breath hitched as I tried to figure out how to respond to that. As I tried to figure out how to comprehend the way he'd asked that.

"Yeah," I said lamely. "That is so."

"Hm." August's eyes stayed firmly on his face, but I sensed a struggle. It was the same struggle I'd already worked through. "Well, I'll leave you to shampoo in peace and without judgment," he said before moving on to give me a rundown of how to work the shower so we wouldn't end up in this situation again.

For some reason, I felt a slight twinge of disappointment at that. And it grew as August moved to leave the shower. Some unhinged part of my brain wanted to reach out and stop him. Worse yet, that part of my brain wanted to ask if he wanted to stay and help me. I had a feeling those large hands of his would do wonders at massaging my scalp.

The same unhinged part of my brain caused me to open my mouth and say, "Next time, I'm going to have to barge into your shower and judge your shampoo skills."

Mischief glinted in August's eyes as he looked over his shoulder. "You're welcome any time."

God, I really wished he hadn't said that.

August stepped out of the shower, saving me from answering. But then he stopped and stared at the ground and the mess his sopping-wet towel was making.

He sighed and glanced back at me again. "Unless you really did want to take notes, you might want to close your eyes. I need to shuck this towel and grab a new one, so I don't drench the floors."

I didn't want to close my eyes, but I did. Because, after all, admiring August Fletcher's naked ass would be unprofessional.

And while I hadn't been successful dancing around those professional boundaries my first twenty-four hours in Evergreen Isle, that didn't mean I couldn't get my shit together tomorrow.

"See ya after your shower," August called, and since his voice echoed, indicating he was further away and likely once again covered, I opened my eyes. "We've got to head into town and get some groceries, so I can cook us dinner tonight."

"You can cook?" I called back.

I could almost feel him roll his eyes in response. "Yes, I can cook. Don't sound so surprised."

With that, he left the bathroom, leaving me to stew in the thick steam.

I wasn't just surprised at what I'd found so far on Evergreen Isle. I was downright shocked.

And most importantly, absolutely screwed.

a/n:

I did say forced proximity, didn't I?

Thanks for reading! xoxo amelie

seven | teamwork

I T HAD BEEN LESS than twenty-four hours since I saw Quinn Castle walk into Sunny's, and I'd already lost my goddamn mind.

I could justify keeping her in my bed last night to ensure she didn't get too sick. And I could justify inviting her out to the beach while she wore that yellow torture device. But barging into her bathroom like that?

What the hell was wrong with me?

Thank fuck she'd been wearing her swimsuit because I was pretty sure if I'd walked in to see Quinn Castle naked in the shower, I wouldn't have known how to function. Looking at her with that wet little bikini plastered to her skin was a challenge enough. Considering how all the blood in my body rushed to my dick the moment I stepped into that bathroom, I'd been so close to giving her a really good idea of those measurements of mine.

Shaking my head in disbelief and disappointment in myself, I opened the refrigerator door to take stock of what was in there before I headed to the store. Just as I finished my mental checklist, Quinn's footsteps alerted me, followed by a loud sigh as she neared the kitchen.

I closed the fridge to find her rounding the corner, wearing loose jeans and a yellow tank top with spaghetti straps and buttons up the front. She looked like the fucking summer sun. And it made me want to jump back into the shower and blast cold water all over my body.

"Was that a sigh of relief?" I asked, cocking a brow. "That you made it out of the shower alive? Maybe I should have stayed to supervise."

I definitely shouldn't have.

Leaving had been the right choice because if I hadn't left...Well, I couldn't think about that. Because Quinn had already eyed up my cock today, and I didn't need it to grow and give her another reason to stare at it.

It liked having her eyes on it way too fucking much.

"No," she snorted. "I'm just relieved that you're–"

She cut herself off, and curiosity got the best of me.

"That I...?"

"Nevermind."

God, she knew just how to keep me frustrated.

"I'm gonna head to the store," I said, deciding not to pester her further. It was probably better that I didn't know what she was going to say.

"I thought we were going to the store."

Yeah, that had been my plan. Until I'd walked out of her shower and back to my room, only to realize how fucking hard it was to be around this woman and keep my head on straight. As soon as I'd closed my bedroom door, I'd replayed what I'd done. What I'd said.

Again, what the hell was wrong with me?

Quinn wasn't here so I could flirt with her. She was here to do her job.

"You don't need to come," I insisted. "I won't be gone long."

"I want to come," she argued. Of-fucking-course, she argued. "It would be good for me to see more of the town. See what just a run-of-the-mill trip to the grocery store is like for you."

I barely resisted rolling my eyes.

Because it would not be a run-of-the-mill trip to the grocery store. Not with Quinn tagging along. Nothing about this arrangement was ordinary. And I didn't know how to act normal with an annoyingly pretty New York reporter following me around. Especially when other people would undoubtedly notice the annoyingly pretty New York reported following me around.

In fact, the more I thought about it, the more I thought she should stay here.

"Are you sure you don't want to...I don't know, curl up with a good book until I return?" I offered, but not feeling entirely hopeful.

Quinn frowned. "As nice as that sounds, I didn't come here for vacation, Fletcher."

"Right," I grunted. "You came here to follow me to the grocery store."

She flashed a megawatt smile at me. "Exactly."

|||

"I can pay for the groceries," Quinn said as soon as we walked into Evergreen Isle's only grocery store.

Like everything on the island, wooden coastal shingles covered the outer walls, giving it a charm that screamed beach town. It wasn't much more than a shack nestled in the main drag of Evergreen, but it was comforting.

"You're not paying for the groceries, Castle."

"Why not?" she countered. "It's the least I can do, considering you're letting me stay with you."

"It's not like you're choosing to be here," I argued. "And you won't be here for that long."

Soon she'd be back off galavanting in New York while wearing all her bright yellow clothes in a sunless office building. Fucking Parker would try to win her over again, and I'd be here, sitting in the white sands of South Carolina.

I was too busy thinking about it to realize that Quinn had gone oddly quiet, and I looked over to find her biting on her lip as we strolled through the first aisle, passing through the jars of jelly and peanut butter.

"What?"

"Oh, nothing." She flashed a wary smile that I didn't believe for a goddamn second. "Just trying to figure out how to secretly pay for dinner."

"Stop trying." I scowled. "It's not going to work."

Call me old fashioned, but when I had dinner with a woman, I took care of it. And while tonight couldn't be further from a date, I still felt like I had a responsibility. To Quinn. To make sure she was taken care of on this little island. She wouldn't be stuck here if it weren't for me. Besides, she was living off the shit salary the Warriors likely paid her while I had more money than I'd ever need.

She wasn't fucking paying.

She tsked, clucking her tongue, and I withheld a groan.

"What now?"

"I think you need to improve your teamwork."

"Teamwork?" I repeated. I must have heard her wrong. "Castle, I led a fucking multi-billion dollar franchise to two Super Bowl wins. I think I know a thing or two about teamwork."

She made a humming noise in the back of her throat while dragging her fingers along the wooden shelves. "Well, if we're going to get through this, and I'm going to get this article written, I need you to work with me. Not against me."

I stared at her, brows drawn. "What does that have to do with letting you pay for dinner?"

She shrugged. "Because we should be working together to make dinner, but you're arguing with me about it."

"I have no problem letting you help me make it."

Although dancing around my kitchen with this summer sun had to be a bad idea. Especially after earlier.

A cheery laugh floated from her lips, brightening the grocery store. "Ah, so it's just the money you're controlling about."

I sighed, pausing in the middle of the aisle. "Castle."

She walked a few paces ahead before realizing I'd stopped. Turning around, she smiled. "Yeah?"

"You're here in my hometown and staying at my house," I said, trying to be as direct as possible. "As you've pointed out, I'm not exactly known for my hospitality. But at least let me try to be a good host."

Her eyes grew round as that smile of hers flickered, unsure. A little surprise, and maybe even regret, coated her irises, but a second later, the amusement was back. She started walking backward down the aisle, almost like she was taunting me to follow her.

And of course I was going to.

"If you want me to write that you were a gracious host in the article, you can just say that," she teased.

I rolled my eyes. "I don't give a flying fuck about what you write in that article."

She faltered. "You don't?"

I shook my head.

"Not at all?"

"Nope."

"Oh."

Shit.

It was my turn to let regret seep into my bones. Because based on her wilting expression, I'd put my foot in my mouth.

And I supposed I couldn't really blame her for being ticked. Writing was her livelihood, and I'd just said I didn't give a flying fuck about it. That was like someone walking up to me and saying they didn't give a shit whether I won or lost games.

"Castle–"

"No, I get it." But she turned the corner of the aisle far too quickly, making me think she was trying to hide her expression from me. I rushed after her, but she'd schooled the look on her face by the time I caught up. "So, what's for dinner?"

"I–"

"Let me guess. It's something on the grill."

I'd wanted to apologize for what I'd said, but she threw me off. Again. When I lifted a brow, she merely shrugged it off.

"You just seem like the grilling type. When men say they can cook, they usually just mean they can stick meat on a hot grate."

Her words were a bit clipped, and I had a feeling she was unconsciously taking little jabs at me because of the big jab I'd taken at her.

I didn't like it.

Not because I cared about what she thought about my cooking abilities. I'd prove her wrong about that soon enough.

No, I didn't like it because it meant Quinn felt defensive. I'd made her feel small when everything about her was oddly larger than life.

So I took the jab without comment.

"You're half right," I allowed.

She pursed her lips, waiting for me to go on.

"I was thinking about making homemade pizza on the grill," I explained. "I have a really nice Pinot in my cellar that would pair great with it on a night like tonight."

Her mouth opened and closed, so I leaned closer to whisper against her ear.

"But if you want to see me slap some meat around, I can do that, too."

She cleared her throat, a rosy flush working up her neck before flooding her cheeks. "Homemade pizza sounds great."

I couldn't help the smile that wormed its way onto my face as I led Quinn to the aisle with the ingredients we needed. "If you have another idea, I'm open to suggestions," I said, glancing over my shoulder at her.

Her lips twitched. "Now you're just trying to prove you can be a good teammate."

"I don't know what you're talking about." I grabbed a bag of mozzarella and tossed it to her. "It comes naturally for me."

Quinn rolled her eyes as she caught the cheese, but I could see how tempted she was to smile. "Pizza sounds good, Fletcher."

"Excellent."

We fell into a natural rhythm after that. Quinn followed me around the store, peppering me with questions about the town. I tried to answer without too much groaning as I grabbed all the items we'd need. And luckily, it was empty enough in the store that I didn't encounter anyone who dared to talk to me.

But that didn't mean there weren't people around who recognized me. People who would undoubtedly run their mouths about the pretty brunette in the grocery store with August Fletcher. And while I didn't care what people thought about me, I didn't like bringing attention to Quinn. She didn't deserve to get sucked into the rumor mill.

Even if, technically, she was a part of it.

Relief washed over me as soon as we returned to my truck. We'd made it through one public outing without causing a scene. I knew it wouldn't be the only one if Quinn truly intended to get a picture of my life here on Evergreen. But for now, it was just the two of us again.

And all I could do was hope that I'd make it through the night without doing something I shouldn't.

a/n:

happy monday! hope you enjoyed another peek into August's mind □

thanks for reading!xoxo amelie

eight | hand modeling

I SPENT THE WHOLE way back to August's beach house thinking about how he didn't care about the article. My article. His article.

How could he not care about what I write about him? Thousands, if not millions, of people will undoubtedly read whatever I put together. and he doesn't care?

Sure, I never got the impression that August was too concerned about his image or his reputation. Having a relatively squeaky clean one came naturally to him. He didn't have any scandals attached to his name. He didn't make outlandish remarks that ended up circulating the internet. He was just a guy who was really fucking good at playing football.

Still, this article would be his last statement on his career. His final chance to tell his story, to help people understand his legacy and why he chose to walk away from it. He didn't care about any of that?

It bothered me. Even though my ultimate goal was to not need to write a retirement expose at all and instead convince August to come back to New York. His dismissal still made me feel insignificant and useless like he was just humoring me and my little article when this was likely the most important piece of my career.

But even more than it bothered me, it confused me.

I understood that August didn't care what other people thought of him, but to not have any interest at all? It baffled me. I wished I could be that self-assured. That dismissive of how the world viewed me.

August seemed to know that he upset me. He hadn't brought it up again, but he had been altogether too nice to me the rest of our grocery trip. I wasn't really a fan. It felt like pity...or something else disingenuous.

But my irritation only lasted until he poured me a glass of that Pinot and started rolling out pizza dough he'd made from scratch.

I hadn't even tasted his cooking yet and I was already regretting making fun of his cooking abilities. Somehow, I had a feeling that this would be the best pizza I'd ever had.

"Can I help with something?"

I didn't like feeling useless. I wanted to be more than the tag-along little reporter who followed the big-shot NFL player around. Retired NFL player, but still.

"I have a brick of parmesan in the fridge. You could grate it."

I nodded, hopping down from the barstool to walk around the kitchen island. I brushed past August as he continued working the dough and didn't miss how his body stiffened at the tiniest contact.

God, this man.

One minute he was pushing his way into my shower, and the next, he was recoiling when I so much as grazed his arm in the kitchen. This was going so well.

After getting the cheese, I looked to August, who wordlessly pointed me to a drawer on the other side of the kitchen. I followed his directions, opening the drawer to find a cheese grater sitting on top of a collection of utensils. I grabbed it before rummaging through his cupboards to find a small bowl. Then I took all the items and went to stand next to August at the counter.

And unless it was my imagination, he seemed to...shrink away from me.

What the hell was going on?

I decided to ignore it, focusing instead on the task he'd given me and trying not to admire the way his hands worked the dough, kneading and pressing it into the perfect crust. With the risk of sounding like a weirdo, I had to admit that August Fletcher had beautiful hands. They were large, rippled with just the right amount of veins, and looked more than capable.

He cleared his voice. "Something wrong with the dough?"

But of course he caught me staring.

"No, it looks great."

"You're inspecting it as though you're just waiting for me to do something wrong."

I laughed and decided to get through this in the easiest way I knew how: turn it into a joke.

"I'm not inspecting the dough at all, Fletcher," I admitted with a slight grin. "I'm just wondering if you realize you could have a career in hand modeling if your other retirement plans, which you won't tell me, don't work out."

His movements slowed, his hands flexing in a way that only made the whole thing that much more erotic. So to combat the way my thoughts were going, I simply kept talking.

"Honestly, it would be perfect," I continued. "A hand model doesn't have to show their face, so no one will even know it's you. It can be an incognito thing if you want, and there are a million online opportunities that would love to have you."

August arched a brow as he looked over at me, his knuckles gradually working to flatten the dough to just the right degree of thickness. "And what kind of things do you imagine my hands to be doing in these...mod eling shots."

Oh, God.

"I mean, I wasn't imagining it," I sputtered.

He lifted his other brow, goading me to tell the truth.

I was starting to think that my assessment of August Fletcher's character had missed a few things, including how his cockiness overshadowed his humility from time to time.

"You can't just feed me ideas without specifics, Castle." His lips twitched, and I realized he was having far too much fun with this even though he was trying–and failing–to keep a straight face. "Am I modeling to sell products? Or am I the product?"

I made a grab for my wine on the countertop. I needed it for support. "Could be either, honestly."

"Well, I need to know if I have to find a modeling partner," he shot back, and the gravel in his voice made warmth run down my spine. I chased it with a gulp of wine. "I could make my hand into a necklace, but I doubt that content would sell unless I have a pretty neck to put it around."

I nearly choked on my wine before staring at his nearly-empty glass. "How much of that wine did you have?"

His eyes twinkled as he looked down at me. "You're the one chugging it."

I put my glass back on the counter with more than enough force. It clanked loudly, and I grimaced, worried for a second that it would break. "Yeah, well, it's hot in here," I said, waving a hand in front of my face.

Despite the airy, open-concept kitchen, the space felt stuffy. Overheated. Like I was a couple seconds away from breaking a sweat even though I was just standing here.

August gave the dough a final smack as though satisfied with the crust he'd made. "The A/C is blasting, and the last time I checked, red wine isn't exactly considered refreshing."

I rolled my eyes, giving him a playful push since he'd bested me into a corner, but I forgot for a moment that he was a massive hulk of a man who didn't so much as budge when I shoved him. My attempt did make him bite down on a smile, though.

"You keep trying to catch me off guard with these little questions of yours, Castle," he said in that gruff voice of his as he turned to face me, leaning one hip against the counter. "But I'm quicker than you give me credit for." He leaned forward, his proximity burning through me as he lowered his pitch. "And if you want to know about my retirement, you'll have to work a little harder than that."

I forced myself to swallow past the dryness in my throat and propped a hand on my hip. "You can at least tell me if I'm hot or cold with the hand modeling thing."

"Cold," he chuckled, leaning back again, allowing me to breathe easier. "Very, very cold."

"Hmm," I considered, giving him a once over. "For a second, it really seemed like you knew what you were talking about."

August reciprocated my look, his eyes flicking up and down my body. At this point, the kitchen didn't just feel warm. It felt downright sweltering.

"Just because I haven't made it a business doesn't mean I don't know what to do with my hands."

I made another grab for my wine glass. "You're talking about football, right?"

"Right, Castle." His lips curved slowly. "I'm talking about football."

I wasn't sure I believed that, but I definitely wasn't about to press it any further. Egging August on when he had that fire in his gaze seemed like a terrible idea, yet it was taking everything in me not to do it.

He cleared his throat. "Now, if you're done staring at my hands, this dough needs some sauce."

"I wasn't staring," I argued. "I was observing."

"Mhm," August murmured before he turned around to grab the pizza sauce from the bag of groceries we brought home.

I sighed and took another sip of my wine, knowing that arguing with him was useless.

I'd been staring. Admiring. Imagining. I'd been doing everything he accused me of. But in defense of my professionalism, teasing August had proved a great way to get him to open up, bit by bit. Sure, maybe I didn't get to the bottom of his retirement, but every opportunity to loosen his tongue had to benefit me in the long run, right?

August and I redirected our conversation to dinner for the next ten minutes. Which was good—pizza was about as safe a topic as possible. I helped sprinkle cheese over the sauce, and August seemed considerably more relaxed than when I first brushed past him in the kitchen. Plus, our conversation in the grocery store about my article had long since disappeared to the back of my mind.

Once it was time for August to whip out the pizza stone and fire up the grill, I let him take over, happy to sit back and watch the man work as I sipped my wine on the deck.

I should be watching the ocean. Or the sunset. Or anything that wasn't the flex of August's muscles as he lifted the cover on the grill, but I starting to realize just how hopeless I was. And considering his back was to me, what was the harm?

The harm, of course, was that eventually he'd turn around and catch me staring. Again.

So I sank lower in my chair and focused instead on the swirling of seagulls along the shoreline until dinner was ready.

We ate outside since it was so nice, and August allowed me to set the table. Honestly, after his little show in the grocery store about wanting to be a good host, I was surprised he even let me help with dinner at all. And then he surprised me yet again when he sat down and threw me an investigative bone.

"I do have a couple business ventures that I've been involved in," he said. "And I'm only telling you this because I have a few calls I'll have to take care of tomorrow. You might be on your own for a bit."

"Do these business ventures involve hand necklaces?" I questioned, cocking my head to the side. "Or why can I not be included in them?"

I might have been imagining things, or perhaps it was the reflection of the sunset, but August's face turned a slight shade of pink. But then he shook his head with a playful–and rare–smile.

"No, Castle. I just don't think you'll find them very interesting."

I leaned forward.

"I think I'll be the judge of that, Fletcher."

a/n:

they're both riding the struggle bus

thanks for reading! xoxo amelie

nine | ceiling wood

I WOKE THE following day with the most severe case of morning wood I'd probably ever had.

I wasn't delusional enough to think it had anything to do with my high morning testosterone levels. No, it had everything to do with Quinn Castle and the thoughts that plagued me when we finally parted ways last night—when I got into my bed and realized that my sheets smelled like her.

They smelled like the fucking sun. I wasn't sure how that was possible, but Quinn smelled like a quintessential summer day. Like creamy coconut with a hint of citrus.

Every time I rolled over, I was reminded of how she'd slept next to me that first night. Her soft little snores and flicker of her long lashes as she drifted into a restless sleep. Her warm body snug beside mine, even though there were blankets, clothes, and everything between us.

But honestly, it was more torturous to have her in the room next door than to have her in my bed. That night she slept next to me, she'd been drunkenly passed out, and all I'd been focused on was making sure she didn't choke on her own vomit. I'd kept myself in check, including my thoughts.

Tonight, though, my mind couldn't help but wander to places it shouldn't. No doubt a result of how my conversations with Quinn always seemed to end in thinly veiled sexual innuendos and close proximities.

God, I wished I could just shut off that part of my brain so we could get through this little interview experience. But it was useless, and all the thoughts I shouldn't be thinking extended into my sleep last night, weaving into my dreams.

That had to be the reason for how fucking hard I was when I woke, thoughts of Quinn on the brain.

I stared at the ceiling, trying to tame the desire to wrap my hand around my cock. It was wrong, so wrong, to do that when Quinn was probably still sleeping on the other side of my bedroom wall. It was even worse to do it while remembering how she'd pressed so close to me in the shower, steam and slick skin all around us.

Fuck.

I stared at the ceiling instead, at the slatted wooden boards covering it. I concentrated on them. On how some of them had little knots disrupting the grain pattern. On how some of the knots were darker than others. And then, once I was finished thoroughly inspecting the slates, I counted them. Forty-nine. There were forty-nine across my bedroom ceiling.

Fuck.

No matter how long I stared at the ceiling, my blood still ran hot. Apparently, ceiling wood was not a cure for morning wood.

But I couldn't put off getting out of bed much longer. I needed to hop on a call soon, so if I wanted to be a good host and ensure Quinn had coffee and breakfast, I had to get up.

Surprisingly, when I padded out into the hallway, the smell of coffee wafted through the air. Sure enough, when I rounded the corner to the kitchen, I spotted an already brewed pot on the countertop.

I did a once-over of the main level of my house, searching for the reporter. But I didn't see her and decided maybe she'd made coffee and then retreated with it back into her room. Either way, I was glad she'd made herself at home and helped herself this morning.

After pouring myself a cup, I wandered to the front windows of the house, wanting to catch a glimpse of the ocean waves. I wouldn't have time to take my board out before my meeting, but I could still admire the swells.

And the almost-naked reporter lying out on my deck.

Jesus Christ.

I nearly spat out my coffee when my eyes landed on Quinn in that tiny yellow bikini. Was she trying to give me a heart attack? Shit, maybe she figured that she'd get out of writing this article and trailing me around all day if she just fucking killed me.

She must have just applied tanning lotion or oil or something because her skin looked so goddamn dewy. She practically shone as she crossed one leg over the other, a cup of coffee in one hand and some kind of reading tablet in the other.

At this point, I should have just stayed in bed, counting the boards on my ceiling.

Although, there probably wasn't any point in bothering with that. Not with Quinn hanging around, wearing that bikini. I seemed doomed to have recurring, spontaneous reactions from now until I finally got rid of her.

I groaned before cursing when my phone buzzed–a reminder that I had a meeting in ten minutes.

A meeting Quinn claimed she wanted to attend. But I'd told her what time the call was, and she didn't seem all that interested now. She seemed way more curious about whatever was happening in that book of hers.

I debated, wondering if I should step onto the deck and remind Quinn about the meeting or leave her to her book. It would be way easier to get through business today with her asking a million questions. Still, at the same time, the sooner she got the answers she was looking for and had material to write about, the sooner she'd be walking out the door and heading back to the big apple.

The sooner I could be free from this fucking torture.

So I grabbed my laptop from the table and stepped out on the deck, sucking in a deep breath.

"Castle."

She jumped slightly at the sound of my voice, twisting in her chair, and dear God, being around her while she wore literal scraps of fabric had to be detrimental to my blood pressure.

She grinned, a slight chuckle leaving her lips that I was sure meant to mock me somehow.

"Well, hello August. Good morning to you, too."

August.

I liked it when she called me by my first name.

I cleared my throat. "I have that meeting in a few minutes if you still want to join."

"Oh!" She jumped again, startled as she glanced down at her watch. I inwardly groaned, trying not to react to how her swimsuit top shifted to a dangerous angle. Dangerous for my fucking sanity. I jerked my eyes to Quinn's face, only to catch her frown. "But I thought the meeting was at ten o'clock."

I shook my head. "No, it's at nine."

Her frown deepened. "I could have sworn you told me it was at ten."

"Definitely didn't. But you don't have to come. I just wanted to remind you in case you were still interested."

"I'm still interested," she said, pushing off the lounge chair. "Even though I'm pretty sure you told me the wrong time as a ploy for me to miss the meeting, and I'm pretty sure you don't want me there."

I raised a brow and sat at the patio table, opening my laptop. "If I didn't want you there, why would I have reminded you about it?"

Quinn's lips drew together in an adorably irritated pout. She ignored my question–likely because she knew I was right. "I'm going to grab my computer to take notes during the meeting. Are you sitting outside for it?"

I nodded and pointed at her sun-tanning spot. "You're welcome to just sit where you were before and listen in."

In other words, as far away from me as physically possible. Because I swore every time we got within a few feet of each other, words came out of my mouth that only made this harder.

Literally.

"You don't want me to introduce myself to anyone?" Quinn cocked her head to the side. "Hop in to let them know I'm technically on the call?"

I understood what she was saying; she wanted transparency around her presence as a reporter who'd be taking notes on the going-ons of our business. But still...no.

"I will let them know you've joined us, but no, I don't want you to...hop in."

I would prefer she did zero hopping, no hopping at all.

Not in what she was wearing.

"Why not?"

"You're wearing a bikini, Castle," I sighed, waving a hand in her general direction while I kept my eyes strictly on the laptop as I found the correct link in my calendar. "I don't need to derail the entire video conference before it begins. The guys are easily distractible."

I felt like a hypocrite saying that, considering how easily distractible I was, too.

Quinn rolled her eyes. "Fine. I will go grab some clothes and my computer. Happy?"

"Sure."

No.

No, I wasn't happy.

Because if Quinn introduced herself to the other guys, even with clothes on, the conversation would likely shift. It was one thing to tell everyone that she was here and another thing entirely to show them. I wouldn't be surprised if they'd seen pictures of Quinn Castle before, but pictures didn't fully convey who she was and how fucking addicting she could be.

The last thing I needed was for other people to get addicted to Quinn, too.

But when Quinn returned to the deck wearing a yellow sundress, she sat at the other end of the table, away from me and the camera. And once everyone had hopped on the call and said their morning pleasantries, she still hadn't moved over to slide into the frame. Relieved, I made to quickly introduce her, so we could move onto business.

"I have a Warriors reporter staying with me this week, and–"

"Oh, is it the one you like?"

Goddamn, Finn. He was one of my best friends and the only one I trusted to partner with on this project. But he didn't fucking know how to keep his mouth shut sometimes.

"Yes," I said tersely, "it's the one I like."

I mean, Quinn must know that I liked her. She was the only reporter I ever let interview me, and while there was a reason for that that went outside who Quinn was as a person, it also had a lot to do with who Quinn was as a person. She had to know I liked her; it wasn't a secret. People brought it up all the time.

They just didn't typically bring it up in front of her.

"What I was going to say was that Ms. Castle is here, listening in on the call," I added, staring at Finn through the computer screen and hoping he'd get the fucking message to close his trap.

"Right..." he muttered before mouthing, "Sorry."

I shrugged, trying not to look at Quinn across the table. I didn't need to know her reaction to that little side conversation. I'd rather pretend it didn't happen.

"So let's get into it," I said, leaning forward onto my elbows.

Besides Finny, there were three other people on the call. Kolson, who was a project manager for the city of Evergreen Isle, and Soren and Zoey, who headed the community's youth programs. Together, we were building a new community sports complex on the island that would target family wellness and open up more youth sports opportunities.

Right now, kids have limited opportunities to play on organized teams and get that kind of exposure to athletics at a young age, and I wanted to change that. And since I was funding it, Kolson, Soren, and Zoey were on board. They'd grumbled a little bit when I insisted on Finn taking the head contractor job instead of the city guy they wanted to use, but ultimately, they gave in.

It was that, or it wasn't happening.

I listened as Finn gave us an update on construction, which was wrapping up this week, and then the five of us talked a bit more about the next steps.

When we wrapped up the call, I closed the laptop to find Quinn giving me a funny look.

"What?"

Her eyes were wide as she mimicked me, closing her laptop slowly.

"How much is all of this costing you?"

I sat back with a frown, crossing my arms over my chest. "I don't want that going in the article."

"Why not?"

"Because I'm not doing this to showboat my wealth or parade how I'm using it to be charitable."

Quinn's expression softened. "That's...very noble of you, August."

August.

There it was again.

Regardless of the way she said my name, my frown deepened. "I'm not doing it to be noble."

"Why are you doing it?"

I sighed.

Quinn had been surprisingly quiet during the meeting. She'd just sat across from me, her keys clicking as she typed rapidly. For a second, I'd imagined I might get away without answering a bunch of questions, but I should have known better.

Too bad I didn't really have time for questions right now.

"Can we talk more about this later?" I asked. "I have to get to Sunny's."

"Oh!" She perked up. "Why are we going to Sunny's?"

God, she was persistent.

"You don't have to come," I said, figuring it was worth a try.

She lifted a brow. "We've been over this."

"Fine," I relented before sweeping my gaze over her sundress. "But wear something that you don't mind getting dirty."

Her lips curved up, and goddamnit, she was going to say something that would make it hard to sleep tonight. I just knew it.

"We gettin' dirty tonight, Fletcher?"

God, I wished.

"Just–" I groaned inwardly, pinching the bridge of my nose. "Go change. We need to leave in fifteen."

She smiled that brilliant smile.

"I'll be ready."

Too bad I couldn't say the same.

a/n:

heading back to the bar. bottoms up!

thanks for reading! xoxo amelie

ten | on wednesdays

I LEFT THE BEACH HOUSE to find August leaning against his jeep, waiting for me.

He tipped his head back when I emerged, and even though I didn't hear him make a noise, he looked like he was groaning. Out of anncyance, I expected. Like he'd half-expected me to change my mind and text him that I was staying at his house.

Honestly, August hadn't complained as much as I thought he would about my presence. I assumed I'd be catching constant flack from him about tagging along to everything he did, but surprisingly, August had kept his mouth shut. Instead, he just glared at me occasionally.

Like he was doing right now, his eyes drifting over my outfit.

Ah, that was why he was annoyed.

"What?" I looked down at what I was wearing: jean shorts and a white tank top. The shorts were old and frayed, and the top wasn't anything special. "You told me to wear something that could get dirty. This was the most casual thing I'd packed."

"Fuck, Castle," August groaned. "You're walking out here like you're ready to win a wet t-shirt contest. Don't any of your clothes have more...clothes to them?"

"It's hot," I protested as sweat trickled down my back as if to back up my point.

When August merely grumbled and turned to get in the car, I bit down on a grin. "You think I'd win though?"

"What?" He frowned, watching as I slid into the passenger seat.

"The wet t-shirt contest. You think I'd win it?"

He shook his head, but I saw the hint of a smile on his lips. "I know you'd win, Castle."

Heat coiled in my lower belly, and I tried to ignore it as I crossed one leg over the other. Before he pulled out of the driveway, I offered, "If you think I should change, I will."

"We don't have time," August said, putting the jeep in reverse. "I'll just have to keep my eye on you tonight."

I pressed my lips together, trying to keep from showing how I felt about that. There was no use lying to myself: I liked August's eyes on me. Maybe I'd have to wear booty shorts more often on this little trip.

"Are you worried I'm going to organize risque contests in the middle of your uncle's bar?"

"I'm not worried about what you're gonna do, Castle." His frown deepened. "It's everyone else I'm worried about."

"Everyone else?" I questioned. "We practically had the whole bar to ourselves on Monday night. I don't think you have a lot to be concerned about, Fletcher."

"That was Monday," he said gruffly while pulling onto the empty road. "Today is Wednesday."

"Thank you for that prolific explanation. I think I just might put that quote in the article."

August shot me a glare, but once again, amusement wasn't too hard to spot in his eyes.

"Is that how you got your job?"

"What do you mean?"

"By being a smartass?"

"Rude." I gasped in mock indignation. "I'll have you know I'm a very capable writer and reporter."

A smile finally wormed its way onto August's face. "I know you are."

The warmth in my belly grew, this time for a different reason.

At least until August added, "I'm just used to a more...professional side of you."

He was right about that. I'd been a far cry from professional since showing up on Evergreen Isle, and I inwardly cringed that August had noticed it, too. Although that shouldn't be a surprise considering I'd already gotten drunk, asked him to rub sunscreen over my back, and wound up sharing a shower with him.

But while I regretted some of those things, I also had to acknowledge that it was working. He might be seeing a different side of me than usual, but I was also seeing a different side of him. Or rather, both sides of him. More sides of him. A better picture of who August Fletcher was. And that would only help me finish this assignment.

I cleared my throat. "You don't like reporters, so I'm trying not to act like one."

Both his brows raised, and hurt flashed across his features. "So this...you...this is an act?"

"No!" I nearly shouted the word in my efforts to reassure him. The last thing I wanted was this reporter-shy athlete to think I was tricking him. "No, I'm just...trying to act more like myself and let my guard down so you feel comfortable around me. I'm sure it isn't exactly fun for you to have me following you around and staying at your house."

He sighed, and I hoped I'd convinced him I was telling the truth. Everything that had transpired in the last forty-eight hours had been unapologetically me. And while I wasn't proud of all of it, it was one-hundred-percent Quinn Castle.

"You don't have to worry, Castle. You don't make me feel uncomfortable. Not like that."

I wanted to question exactly what he meant by not like that, but I didn't dare, considering how locked his jaw looked. So instead I teased him, hoping I could melt him back out a bit.

"Is that why you like me?" I asked.

Maybe if I made it into a joke, I could stop thinking about the strange rush of adrenaline that flooded me when August's friend asked if I was the reporter he liked, and he, so ridiculously casual about it, admitted yes.

Sure, I knew August Fletcher didn't hate me like the rest of my colleagues, but to admit that he liked me? Well, let's just say I hadn't expected to hear that. Even if he did only mean it in a platonic, I-can-tolerate-you sort of way.

"Yes, Castle." August's lips curved in a gentle smile even as he rolled his eyes. "That's why I like you."

I wanted to tease him more but decided against it. I liked this moment. I wasn't entirely sure why, but I liked it. And I didn't want to mess it up. So I fell silent, rolling down the window and reveling in the ocean air as it slapped me across the face. I breathed in, loving how it smelled while I watched the scenery pass us by on the way to the island bar.

When August held the door open at Sunny's for me to step inside, I realized he was right. For whatever reason, a Wednesday afternoon at Sunny's was way busier than a Monday night. Every table looked occupied, and at least half a dozen people were waiting in the entryway as they tried to snag a spot. The smell of grease and sea food wafted through the air.

August's fingers wrapped around my right hip, and I tried to control my breathing as his touch burned through my clothes. But it was no use. A moment later, his chest pressed against my back, a hot wall of muscle propelling me through the crowd.

"On Wednesdays, Sunny hosts a fish fry," he grunted in my ear, his hands working to maneuver me in the direction he wanted. Honestly, it was a miracle I was able to follow his lead and stay on my feet considering how close he was. And how husky his voice sounded when his lips flirted with my ear. "Starts at one and lasts until closing. It's all hands on deck 'round here on Wednesdays. The whole damn town will make an appearance at some point today."

August did not sound excited about that last part. I found it ironic that a man who made a living performing for massive crowds hated being in them.

I let August guide me behind the bar where Sunny and a tall man with beachy blonde hair were slinging drinks for patrons who'd sidled up to the bar. Sunny nodded at us but didn't pause for small talk.

The same couldn't be said for the other man, who stopped what he was doing when he saw August and me standing at the end of the back bar. He threw a towel on his shoulder and regarded us with a cool, toying grin that slunk its way onto his face while he popped a hip against the counter.

"Look who decided to show up."

August cleared his throat. "Had a busy morning."

The man's brows did a little wiggle, and I could tell he was about to make a joke that would make me flush when August cut in.

"Cohen, this is Quinn. She's a Warrior's reporter. She's gonna hang around today. Quinn, this is my cousin, Cohen."

I stuck my hand out with a smile, happy to meet someone else in August's life. He'd mentioned how he helps out at the bar with his cousin, and this was the perfect opportunity to experience one of the reasons that August had returned to the Isle when he could have retired anywhere in the world.

Cohen gripped my hand, returning my greeting.

"Welcome to the fun, Quinn."

"Thank you!" I replied breathlessly. "I'm happy to be here and will help however possible."

Cohen nodded, exuding warmth as he continued to shake my hand until August cleared his throat. I dropped from Cohen's grip to look over my shoulder, finding August dragging a stool toward me.

"Sit," he said, pointing to it.

I gave him a look. "I'm not a dog."

Although I'd sit if it meant he'd call me a good g—

"I'm well aware," August said dryly, eyes flicking over me. "But I need you to sit in a spot that's out of the way while I–"

"If you want me to stay out of the way, I can just find a spot along the bar to–"

"If I'm on this side of the bar, you're on this side of the bar," he argued, his hard voice telling me he wouldn't back down. "Not letting you out of my sight, remember?"

"I think you'll still be able to see me if I'm across from you." I lifted a brow. "Better than if I'm behind you."

"Castle," he groaned my name like he'd done earlier when I walked out of the house. "Just–"

"Fine," I broke in because I could tell I was stressing him out, which was the opposite of my intention. "I'll stay on this side of the bar. But then at least let me help. It's packed in here."

"I don't have time to teach you the ropes."

I scanned the bar, watching Cohen and Sunny fill beer after beer with a flick of the tap before looking back at August.

"Pretty sure I can handle pouring some drinks," I said, snatching a spare towel off the countertop and tucking it into the back pocket of my jean shorts. Ignoring the look on August's face, I brushed past him and leaned toward a waiting patron.

"What can I get you?"

Behind me, I heard August swear under his breath.

Meanwhile, I grinned.

I had a feeling I was going to have fun today.

a/n:

I think August is definitely regretting bringing Quinn to Sunny's. And the night's just getting started!

xoxo amelie

eleven | old fashioned

" **A** N OLD FASHIONED."

I wiped a few beads of sweat off my brow with the back of my hand and then turned toward the gruff voice at the end of the bar.

Ah, it was my favorite grumpy, tropical Santa Claus. Given his lack of manners when he'd announced his order like a demand, I should have known it was the innkeeper.

I smiled at Mark. "Hi there."

He grunted in reply, and I wondered if maybe he didn't remember me. But then, after a long pause, he raised a brow. "Makin' yourself at home, huh?"

"Sure am." My grin widened as I wiped off the bartop before him, ridding it of residual spilled beer. "Might as well make myself useful while I'm here."

He gave a succinct nod. "How 'bout you make yourself useful and make me an old fashioned."

Just as lovely as always.

"Be nice to our guest, Mark."

I felt August's presence before I heard him. He hovered behind me, similar to how he'd been hovering the whole day. And while I didn't mind having him close, having his arms brush mine when he reached around me to grab something, it made it awfully hard to form coherent thoughts. Or to pour glasses of beer without spilling.

""Scuse me," Cohen muttered, sliding behind us as he grabbed another glass, forcing August to step even closer. His arms caged around me as he leaned on the countertop, and his hard, broad chest grazed across my back.

"I'll get you your old fashioned," August said to Mark. His lips had to be just above my ear, his breath fanning against my skin as he looked at Mark over my shoulder.

Mark nodded his thanks. Well, I wasn't entirely sure if he was saying thank you, but I decided to pretend he was. It made me dislike him less.

"I can get it," I said to August, facing him.

That had been a mistake.

August still hadn't stepped away, meaning his face was only inches from mine. And God, was it a handsome face. I could see all the little bits of stubble in his five o'clock shadow and had to resist the urge to run my fingers over it, just to see what it felt like against my skin.

And then he spoke in that deep, husky voice of his, and I nearly melted into a puddle on the floor.

"You're good at slinging at beers, I'll give you that, Castle." His lips twitched in what I suspected was amusement. Or at least I hoped it was. He dropped his voice even lower before continuing. "But Mark here is a little...uh, particular."

I could only imagine.

I ducked under August's arm, afraid that if he stood that close to me any longer, I'd simply cease to exist. I grabbed a tumbler from the counter and then searched for the rest of my ingredients: bitters, simple syrup, orange peel, Makers.

A quick glance over my shoulder told me that August was watching me with keen eyes. He leaned against the bar, ignoring the chaos behind him and the five people trying to get his attention to order a drink. Although truth be told, I didn't even need to look back to know he was staring. I could feel his gaze following my every move as I got to work.

He wasn't kidding when he said he was going to keep an eye on me.

"Good thing an old fashioned is my specialty, then," I said, giving him a wink.

He shook his head slowly, trying not to smile as he did. He brushed past me, leaning down to whisper in my ear. "All I'm saying is don't come crying to me when he's an ass."

I looked over at him as he poured a beer for the guy impatiently tapping his credit card on top of the bar. "You have such little faith in me, Fletcher."

"No," he said, keeping his eyes on the beer. "It has nothing to do with you. I'm sure most people would love your old fashioned." He dropped his voice to muffle his words even though the volume in the packed bar was almost unbearably loud. "But Mark is not most people."

"Oh, I know," I assured him, mimicking his focus as I kept my eyes trained on my glass and the whiskey I was pouring into it. "We had a lovely first meeting."

"Ah, that's right," August muttered as I watched him run the man's card out of the corner of my eye. When he was done, he closed the distance between us and found my ear to whisper in again. "If you want to poison the man because he's responsible for you having to stay with me, might I suggest you don't do it with dozens of witnesses?"

I spared a glance at August, steeling myself for his smokey gaze. Sure enough, there it was. Boring a hole straight into me.

"Maybe that was why I wanted to make the drink," I countered. "Because I was worried you'd poison him for the very same reason."

August rolled his eyes as he stepped back again. "You've got it all wrong, Castle."

I gave him a disbelieving look before adding the finishing touches on my old fashioned. "Do I?"

August didn't answer. He simply crossed his arms over his chest and watched me bring the drink to Mark, who looked at it with heavy judgment. I had a feeling that Mark was the kind of guy who had only ever had three people make an old fashioned for him–August, Sunny, and Cohen. And I bet he didn't even know how to make one himself.

I held my breath as Mark lifted the drink to his lips. My parents had a wet bar at their house, and my dad was a self-taught mixologist who'd passed me a few tips for the more straightforward and well-loved drinks. When I went to college, I sort of fell in love with it, too. Mixing drinks in the back of frat houses became my best party trick.

Both of Mark's brows shot up as soon as he took a drink, and then a satisfactory nod followed. There might have even been a hint of a smile. It was hard to tell.

"Good."

One word, but I'd take it. Good.

I flashed August a triumphant grin, and he was already shaking his head with disbelief. A ghost of a smile played on his lips, and his heavy-lidded gaze landed on me, telling me things I didn't fully understand.

He sighed. "What am I gonna do with you, Castle?"

I crossed the space and poked him in the chest. "I think the main thing you've learned here is not to underestimate me, Fletcher."

He chuckled. "Never."

It went on like that for the rest of the afternoon. We worked in unbearably close quarters to ensure everyone was well-supplied with drinks while Sunny mostly handled the food, ushering trays between the cooks in the kitchen and the crowded tables. Cohen bounced back and forth between the bar and the kitchen, checking in with us whenever it got too busy. And August glared at the poor men who attempted to flirt with me while I poured them a drink.

Around the time the sunset blazed through the windows, casting a pinkish glow over the bar, August grabbed me by the wrist and tugged me toward an empty table. The rush had died down, leaving us with a few spare minutes, and I happily plopped into an open chair, giving my aching feet a rest.

"Sit." He put a glass of water before me, followed by a beer and a basket of fried food. "Drink. Eat."

August Fletcher had always been a man of fewer words, but even this was a bit more utilitarian than I was used to. I looked up to find his brow beaded with sweat and his eyes tired.

"You," I said, patting the chair next to me. "Sit. Drink. Eat."

That got a thread-bare laugh out of him, but he just shook his head and stalked away, returning to his place behind the bar.

I shrugged, deciding not to let the food go to waste. I bit into a hot French fry and damn near moaned out of delight and hunger. It was just as good as drunk-me remembered. After washing it down with a sip of beer, I relaxed into the chair, letting my eyes drift over Sunny's. They caught on a man with loose, jet-black curls. A man who was walking directly toward me.

When he didn't so much as slow down as he neared, I straightened in my seat, eying him cautiously.

Maybe August had been right about not letting me on this side of the bar.

"You must be the reporter," the man said as he invited himself to sit beside me. "I know everyone in this bar besides you, so I'm guessing you're Quinn."

I relaxed when I heard his voice because it was one I hadn't been able to forget it. Not after it had said, "Oh, is it the one you like?" earlier today. I couldn't forget that.

I grinned as I wiped my hands off on a napkin. "And you must be Finny."

He matched my grin, clearly pleased that I'd figured that out so quickly.

Call it my other party trick—being able to match voices.

"I'm surprised Auggie left you sitting here alone," he said, plucking a fry from my basket without asking. I pushed it forward, indicating I was more than willing to share.

I swallowed a laugh. "Well, I think it was either that or watch me pass out from hunger."

Finny pushed the basket of fries back toward me. "Oh shit."

I shook my head with a smile. "No, please have some. I'm fine." Finn responded by flashing me a doubt-filled look, so I insisted. "Really."

With a shrug, Finn plucked another fry from the basket and resumed his munching, giving me a chance to get a good look at him. He was handsome. Not as handsome as August, granted, but he had a similar ruggedness to him, which made sense considering he was a contractor. Like August, he looked like the kind of man who worked with his hands and didn't mind directing other people who did the same.

"So, how long are you in town?" he asked after a beat of silence.

God, I hated that question. The uncertainty of it. "Until I'm not, I suppose."

A sly grin slipped onto Finny's face. "I bet August loves that."

I flicked my eyes up–a slight roll. "Oh, I'm sure he does."

Finny chuckled. "I wasn't being sarcastic."

My stomach flipped at his implication. But I knew that couldn't be true. Even if heat occasionally flickered between us, I was a pain in August's ass. Plain and simple.

But speaking of heat...

I risked a glance over at August only to find his eyes on me. I'd felt them. They'd announced themself loud and clear when they landed on the side of my face, causing a blush to work up into his cheeks. It was unnerving.

I quickly looked back to Finn, unable to handle the glare August was giving us.

Finny wore a smirk that told me he was the troublemaker of the group. And it also told me he was enjoying this.

"I bet he'd love it if I asked you to dance, too," he said, jerking his head behind us to the floor that had been cleared for an evening of dancing. Someone must have been manning the jukebox I found a couple nights ago because it had been blaring hit after hit for the past hour.

I lifted a brow. "No sarcasm, right?"

He laughed, his curls bouncing as he tossed his head back.

"All the sarcasm." He nodded toward the food in front of me. "But finish eating first."

It didn't escape notice that he hadn't actually waited for my reply on if I even wanted to dance and briefly wondered what it was like to be that confident in life.

Curiosity was what was going to get me tonight. I could feel it in my bones. Because even though I didn't really care to dance with Finny, I sure wanted to see what would happen if I did. After all, I was here to experience Evergreen Isle. And this seemed to be the thing to do on Wednesday nights.

So, a couple minutes later, I let Finn guide me onto the dance floor. His eyes twinkled with a friendliness that put me at ease, and I laughed as he grabbed my hand and twirled me across the floor.

He twirled me so hard that I landed in another man's arms.

Arms I knew immediately belonged to a certain grumpy, retired football player.

a/n:

fun fact: dance scenes are my favorite

thanks for reading!xoxo amelie

twelve | dancing & other activities

"THIS IS WHY I wanted to keep you on my side of the bar."

August's husky voice overtook my senses as he murmured in my ear. He'd caught me in his arms, trapping me with my back to his chest. We were both covered in a light sheen of sweat, so I probably should have been uncomfortable with how close we were, but August curled around me protectively, and I didn't care to break away.

Once I'd recovered from the surprise of running into him, I glanced over my shoulder. His eyes glittered like hard diamonds, ever watchful.

"I'm not allowed to dance?" I asked.

"You're allowed to dance," he murmured before his eyes darted past me, presumably to his friend. "Just not with Finny."

I looked across the dance floor to find Finn watching us, a sly grin on his face.

"I don't think he even really wanted to dance with me," I said honestly.

Pretty sure it was just a tactic to make this happen, which made me wonder how much August's friends knew about me. I'd assumed when August had mentioned that he liked me, he simply meant in comparison to other reporters. But now...

"I wouldn't be so sure about that," August grunted.

He still hadn't released me, which was surprising. But not as surprising as when August began swaying his hips to the beat of the sultry music coming from the jukebox in the corner by the pool table. Without thinking, I mimicked his movements, letting us sway together.

"Fine, then tell me who else is on the no-dance list," I said, following his lead and dropping my weight against his sturdy wall of muscle, letting him take control. "What about that guy?"

I pointed to a man sitting on the edge of the dance floor. He had beachy blonde hair and the look of someone who'd had one too many beers. I'd see his eyes flit over me a number of times throughout the past few hours. I didn't think it was in interest, though. More...curiosity. Like he wanted to know who I was and where I came from. And similarly, I was curious who he was and if he had a reason to care.

August's grip tightened around my waist, his tone tinted with warning. "You don't even know that guy."

"So?" I shrugged, smiling to myself.

I couldn't see August's face, but I imagined him rolling his eyes.

"No."

"What?"

"I'm answering your question. No, you're not allowed to dance with him."

"Because I don't know him?"

"Yes." August paused before finishing his answer. "You shouldn't dance with people you don't know."

"I don't know anyone in this bar besides you," I commented lightly.

"Guess that means you're dancing with me, then." But despite his words, August's arms slowly loosened as he settled his hands on my hips instead. He heaved a sigh. "Or we can sit back down."

This man really loved to tell me to sit today. But even though my feet ached, and my legs were killing me from working the bar all day, I didn't feel like resting. The music was infectious, and the closeness of August's body was equally addictive. Other bar-goers crammed around us, similarly drawn by the atmosphere and good music.

"Sit?" I questioned. "You're not going to dance with me, Fletcher?"

I flashed him a small smile over my shoulder, catching a glimpse of his hardened expression. It was difficult to read, but I thought I detected indecision.

He didn't want to sit down, either.

"It's not a good idea," he said with a frown, even as his fingers dug into my hips, reluctant to let go. The song changed, the tempo picking up, and he followed it, demanding my body to move, too. I could tell how much he liked taking control. How much he craved it. The faster pace felt dirtier, like we were chasing something and couldn't wait to reach it.

"Why not?" I asked breathlessly.

August's breathing had picked up, too. I could feel his rough gasps on the shell of my ear as he tried to devise a reason why it wasn't a good idea.

I knew why. It was because of this. This felt good. Too good. This felt like something we really shouldn't be doing. Something undeniably unprofessional.

"I'm supposed to be behind the bar," he rasped eventually.

"The rush is over," I reasoned as I looped my arm back, hooking it behind his neck. I didn't want him to go. Not yet. Not when this felt like a perfectly good excuse to keep him close to me. This wasn't definitely wasn't a good idea. But it felt too good to stop, and I could say this whole thing was for the sake of the experience. Right? "They'll survive without you for one song."

August released a breath, a hot sigh that had me repressing a shiver. "One song," he allowed.

"One song," I agreed.

One song, and then we'd put a stop to this. He'd go back behind the bar, and I'd return to my lone table, and we'd keep a little distance between us. I would need that if I even hoped to survive this trip.

We fell silent for a bit, letting the music take the lead. August wrapped an arm around me again, pulling me flush to his chest before trailing his other hand up my arm, still hooked around his neck. I could feel the worn calluses on his fingertips as they brushed over my skin, and the roughness made my senses tingle. Every light touch felt seductive, although I was sure he didn't mean it that way. In fact, I was starting to suspect that August Fletcher was simply an experienced man on the dancefloor.

When August's touch disappeared, I dropped my tingling arm. I shouldn't encourage this, although I wondered if it was too late. My arm wasn't the only thing tingling, and my skin was feverish. Every rock of August's body against mine felt like a tick on a timebomb.

"You're a good dancer." I cleared my throat, glancing back at him. His face remained stoic, tense. "Do you do this often? Dance the night away at Sunny's?"

I felt him shake his head. "Never."

My brows raised. "You don't dance?"

Another shake of his head.

"You could have fooled me," I commented because August Fletcher knew how to move. It shouldn't surprise me, considering the coordination and talent he displayed during football games, but still. There was a difference between knowing how to catch balls and knowing how to use your own to catch women in a hold like he had me in. A hold that felt delicious.

"It's just rhythm, Castle," he said gruffly. "And there are other...activities that practice rhythm. Activities I'm pretty damn good at."

The low, husky way he'd muttered those last words couldn't be a mistake. "Activities, huh?"

I had a feeling I knew what activities he was talking about, and I didn't doubt he was good at them. August rarely uttered a cocky word, so whenever he did, there was something undeniably sexy about it.

"I can spell it out for you if you want," he offered, and I could hear the smirk in his voice.

Someone was a bit of a flirt tonight. And frankly, I adored it. Whenever I got August to loosen his tongue a little, I felt accomplished.

"You mean it's not football?"

I couldn't help it; I threw my arm back again, daring to sift my fingers into the soft curls at the base of August's neck. He stiffened momentarily, his hand on my hip flexing as though mimicking how my fingers moved, but then he took his other arm and slid it across my ribcage, encouraging me to lean back into him. I did, resting my head on his shoulder and glancing at him.

This time, he wore a tilted smile as he looked down at me.

"Not football, Castle."

"Good to know," I said, my lips twitching. "I wouldn't want to wrongly credit football for your dancing skills in my article."

His eyes rolled up and then returned, meeting mine with a surge of heat. "You won't write about my dancing skills in your article."

His words were confident, causing me to raise a brow in question. "How can you be so sure?"

"Because then you'd have to explain how you know," he said, lifting a brow back at me. "You'd have to explain this."

He emphasized precisely what this was by grinding his hips into mine, making the rhythm we were following even dirtier. Then he let his fingertips trail across my rib cage, dancing just below my breasts. God, it made me ache. And if I wasn't mistaken, I could feel how equally affected August was.

I bit down on my lip to keep a desperate sound in. When August said he was a grower, he hadn't been lying.

"Definitely wouldn't want to explain this," I gasped when I got a handle on myself.

"That's what I thought," August said smugly.

To my dismay, he eased up, putting a bit of distance between his crotch and my ass, and it was embarrassing how disappointed I was. But if I could get under August's skin once, I could do it again.

"So when's the last time you practiced this...activity?" I asked, flicking my eyes up to his face.

His lips twitched as though he was holding in laughter. "Yesterday."

"Yesterday?" I repeated. "When? With who?"

We had to be thinking about different activities, right? Because if not...well, no. It couldn't be. I'd been with August constantly since I arrived on Evergreen.

Except for when we went to bed last night...

"I don't know why you sound jealous, Castle." August's low voice, suddenly smooth with a hint of amusement, cut into my thoughts. "You were there, and you refused to join.

What the hell was he talking about?

"I think I would have remembered if you had propositioned me yesterday."

"On the beach," August supplied. If he realized how I didn't deny feeling jealous, he didn't say anything. Which was likely for the best, considering how hot my cheeks suddenly felt. "You really don't remember that?"

Dropping my arm from around his neck, I spun in his arms until we faced each other. Confusion riddled my thoughts, and I needed to see his face to fully understand what the hell he was talking about.

"No, I don't. And I think I would remember you asking me to do that on the beach," I said.

His smile was fully formed now. "Asking you to do what, exactly?"

My eyes skirted away from his, evasive, and then August did something I didn't expect. He laughed. It was so full of life that I could feel it vibrating through my body. "Didn't realize Quinn Castle had such a dirty mind," he chuckled. "But I was talking about surfing. It's all in the hips, after all."

He rocked his hips against mine, which had stopped moving, too focused on our conversation.

Goddamn him.

My lips pulled into an embarrassed frown. "I hate you."

He shook his head. "No, you don't."

"How would you know?" I challenged.

His hips once again chased mine. He leaned forward, finding my ears and letting his lips graze the skin just below it. "You weren't dancing with me like you hate me."

He was right about that.

I couldn't help it: I leaned into him and let my body find the rhythm of the music again. It was a different song. We'd said only one, but it was definitely a different song. A slower one, like some kind of ballad.

"And how am I dancing with you?" I asked, keeping my voice low.

I barely heard it, but a moan slipped through August's lips. "I'm really trying not to think too hard about that right now, actually."

I grinned up at him. "Ah, is that why you're so chatty? You need a distraction?"

He shrugged. "Maybe."

Well, if that was the case...I stopped talking and let our bodies pick up where our mouths had left off. But August saw right through me.

He lifted a brow. "Oh, so you want me to think about it?"

It was my turn to shrug. "Maybe I just want payback."

His eyes momentarily fluttered shut. "It's not much of a punishment, Castle."

It took a second for his words to fully seep into my bones, and then I felt them, hot and heady. They weighed me down, grounding me. But not more than a second after my full realization, August abruptly dropped me from his grasp and stepped away with a curse.

Without meeting my eyes, he grumbled, "I have to go back to the bar."

And then he was gone, his absence hitting me hard.

Too hard, considering the circumstances.

I had a sinking suspicion I'd been right; dancing had been something we really shouldn't have done.

a/n:

Respectfully, I disagree, Quinn.

thanks for reading! xoxo amelie

thirteen | castle on a cloud

QUINN FELL ASLEEP on the way back from Sunny's. Considering it was only a ten-minute drive, it was a good indication of just how tired she must be.

I should have made her take a break way earlier than I did. There was no reason she should have been hustling as hard as the rest of us, even though Sunny had commented more than once that having an extra set of hands had been a godsend today.

I told him not to get used to it; Quinn would return to New York before we knew it. He hadn't been impressed by that response, and now I worried that my uncle was planning to kidnap a Warriors reporter just so Wednesdays were a little more bearable.

As for me, I thought today was incredibly unbearable.

Every time Quinn's body brushed against mine, my own body reacted. The slow simmer beneath my skin grew hotter. And even though being near Quinn Castle felt like ongoing torture, I was getting far too accustomed to being burned. Far too accustomed to leaning in to whisper in her ear, brushing my lips across her skin. Far too accustomed to trailing my fingers along her back. Far too accustomed to having her body pressed against mine.

Because that dance...what the hell was that dance?

I should be somewhat consoled that Quinn clearly enjoyed herself as much as me, but I couldn't find it in me. I had a hunch that Quinn viewed dancing and flirting with men in bars as a casual, routine event. But there was nothing about that dance that felt casual to me. It felt like I wanted this woman. Badly.

Always had, but wanting her when I only saw her in small doses during stuffy interviews was manageable. This, though? This did not feel manageable. This did not feel right. She was here for a job, and I'd brought her to my family's bar, acted like a jealous fool when she started dancing with another man, and then encouraged her to grind up against my hard cock.

Fuck, what was I doing?

I glanced to the other side of the car, noting how moonlight cast across Quinn's pretty features as she leaned her head against the window. Her expression was soft and vulnerable, which did nothing to ease the guilt plaguing me.

Quinn Castle was young and carefree, still navigating the earlier days of her career. There was no reason washed-up men like me should be dancing with pretty girls like her in a bar.

Besides, I hadn't forgotten what she said earlier today.

You don't like reporters, so I'm trying not to act like one.

She claimed she wasn't putting on an act, and to an extent, I believed her. But it didn't change the fact that there were things she wanted from me, and part of my brain wondered if she danced with me, flirted with me, and laughed with me because she thought this was how she had to act for me to give them to her.

The chemistry, the heat...that had to be real, though. Didn't it? There was no way that was fake. It couldn't be. I heard her breath hitch, felt her body react to my touch.

Still, this wasn't right. It wasn't how I'd meant for things to go. I'd gotten carried away, and now I needed to fix it.

Quinn didn't stir when I parked my jeep in the driveway, so I walked around the car to carefully open the passenger door. She jolted a bit, sleepily rubbing her eyes, but I murmured for her to go back to sleep before slipping my arms beneath her and scooping her from the seat.

It was better for the both of us if she didn't wake up. Something told me that when Quinn regained full consciousness, she would start peppering me with questions about what happened earlier when I abruptly exited the dance floor, and I didn't know what to say yet.

How was I supposed to tell her that I started thinking too much about exactly how we were dancing, which became very hard to handle. Very, very hard.

Quinn happily readjusted in my arms, letting me carry her inside. She curled into my chest, almost like she was comfortable enough to sleep in this position all night long. I probably wouldn't mind it either, but we'd already had one morning when she woke up in my bed after going to Sunny's. We didn't need another.

Quinn barely stirred as I carried her to the guest bedroom. Only once I set her down on the mattress did she turn, her eyes fluttering open. She squinted at me, and I couldn't help a smile from worming its way onto my face.

"Go back to sleep," I whispered, pulling the blanket over her curled-up body.

"I'm still wearing clothes," she said groggily. "We talked about this, or did you forget?"

Did I forget our conversation a few mornings ago when she gave me permission to take off her clothes if she ever wound up drunk in my bed again? No, I definitely hadn't forgotten that.

But I didn't dare mention anything involving Quinn taking her clothes off. Not after the night we had. And she wasn't drunk. She was just tired, and I'd been really trying to avoid waking her up.

"You're wearing shorts," I said after clearing my throat. "I figured those would be more comfortable than last time when you were wearing jeans."

"Yeah, but they're jean shorts." Quinn groaned before her hands disappeared beneath the covers. She wiggled in the bed, and I wasn't sure what was going on until she whipped her shorts out from under the blanket and tossed them on the floor.

Great. Excellent. Perfect.

Now Quinn Castle was lying in the bed before me, wearing nothing but her underwear and a tank top. It was time for me to leave and try not to think about this or the raging erection I had earlier while in my own bed.

"That's better," she mumbled before turning over and snuggling into the pillow.

It was not better.

"Actually." She turned onto her back again, facing the ceiling as her hands disappeared beneath the covers for a second time. My brain was too mesmerized from watching her body writhe beneath the sheets to realize what she was doing. It should have been obvious, but I was too distracted to expect her to fling her underwear on the ground by my feet, right next to her jean shorts.

It was a black, lacy thong.

"Castle," I groaned.

"What?" she muttered, all innocent and unaware of the pain she was putting me through. "It was sweaty and uncomfortable."

I focused on taking a deep breath, shoving my hands into my pockets.

She misunderstood my silence.

"I promise I'll wash the sheets before I leave," she said.

I must be really fucked up tonight because all I could think about was how I wasn't looking forward to her leaving, and I didn't give a shit if she washed her sheets. More of my house could smell like her, and I'd be fine with that.

"I'm not worried about that," I admitted gruffly. "But if you wanted to wait till I leave next time before stripping your clothes off, that might be good."

"Didn't realize I would offend your delicate sensibilities." She yawned before giving me a tiny, mischievous smile. It seemed like all she could muster in her exhaustion. "Sorry, Fletcher."

"It's fine," I said, sighing before I turned to leave.

"I'm sorry about earlier," she whispered, stopping me in my tracks. "If I...if it was too–"

"I'm sorry, too," I said, cutting her off as I looked over my shoulder. "I shouldn't have–"

"No," she interrupted, her eyes glittering through the darkness as she looked up at me. I hadn't bothered turning on the lamp in the bedroom, so the only sliver of light came from the hallway. "I'm glad you did. I didn't want to dance with Finn. That's not why I went out on the dance floor."

I held my breath at her words, and then decided we should end this conversation before it traveled somewhere dangerous again.

"Quinn, go to sleep."

She blinked at me. Once. Twice. And if she realized I'd used her first name for once, she didn't say anything. She also didn't go back to sleep like I told her to.

"I know you're tired," I continued. "Please rest. I might be gone when you get up. I have a shipment coming in for the sports complex, and I need to be there to unload it early."

"What time?" she asked with another yawn. "I want to come."

"You don't need to."

"It's my job," she countered, which oddly stung.

She's hanging out with you because it's her job, I reminded myself. It shouldn't sting to hear it. I knew it. I knew it all too well.

I sighed. "I need to be there at seven."

She nodded before her eyes fluttered shut again, ready to float off on a cloud of dreams. "Don't leave without me. I want to come."

"Okay, Castle," I relented before leaving the room and gently closing the door behind me. I had a feeling Quinn would be passed out cold within a few minutes. And I had an even greater feeling that I would spend the rest of the night counting the wooden beams on my ceiling.

Yes, she was hanging out with me because it was her job. And yes, she was being paid to be here. But something else she said would replay in my head all night long.

I didn't want to dance with Finn. That's not why I went out on the dance floor.

She wanted to dance with me. That or she wanted to see how easy it was to get a rise out of me. She wanted to see just how tightly she had me wrapped around her pretty little finger.

The answer was very tightly.

The minute Finny had walked over to her table, I'd known he was about to cause trouble. He was my best friend, but hell, did he like to fuck with me. I didn't take my eyes off the two of them for more than a few seconds while they chatted with annoyingly big grins on their faces. And so I caught the very moment Quinn had risen from her chair and followed my friend toward the crowd of bodies.

And then I hadn't even stopped to think. I just moved. I let my feet carry me until she was within reach, and then Finny all but twirled her straight into me. Because he knew that's what I wanted.

And maybe he knew that's what Quinn had wanted, too.

Tired of wrestling with my thoughts, I decided to focus on my body instead. I tossed my shirt into the hamper as I entered my room, walking straight to my bathroom, twisting the faucet in the shower, and cranking it as cold as it would go.

But not even a cold shower seemed to help me tonight.

Showers made me think of Quinn, too. Think of how she'd looked with water running down her smooth skin, with that bikini plastered to her tits, so perfect it was unbelievable.

My shower wasn't safe. My bed wasn't safe. Sunny's wasn't safe.

I suspected I would be living in dangerous territory from here on out. And all I could do was pray I survived Quinn Castle's presence.

Maybe I should just tell her everything. Get this over with. We could sit down, and I could give her every juicy detail she wanted to know about why I left football. About why I was here and what I was doing with my life.

But there was one little problem.

The truth–the full truth–was something she'd never be able to report on.

Not if she wanted to keep her job.

a/n:

he just likes her a *little* bit

thanks for reading!xoxo amelie

fourteen | deflated balls

QUINN DIDN'T STIR when I knocked on her door at six-thirty, and I almost left her behind.

She'd be pissed, but I refused to peek into her bedroom and wake her knowing she'd gone to bed half-naked. No way. I couldn't risk walking in and seeing things I shouldn't see. I couldn't risk the chance of getting yet another boner when I had shit to do that didn't involve ogling my house guest.

Just as I grabbed my car keys from the kitchen counter and was about to walk out the door, Quinn raced down the hallway, wearing leggings and an oversized Warriors T-shirt.

"You were going to leave without me," she accused breathlessly as soon as she saw the keys in my hand.

"You were sleeping," I said simply. I rocked up onto the balls of my feet, trying to stretch. I was stiff today, my body aching. Especially my bad knee. "I didn't want to wake you."

I actually didn't mind the idea of waking Quinn, which was the whole problem. Because the ways I imagined waking Quinn up were...not things I should be thinking about.

Quinn scoffed. "I told you to—never mind. Let me just throw my shoes on, and I'll be ready to go."

She'd pulled her dark hair up into a ponytail on the top of her head, and it swished back and forth as she speed-walked across my living room to retrieve her gym shoes from by the back door. And through the swishing of her hair, I spotted something that made my whole body tighten.

My name.

She was wearing a Warriors shirt with my name on the back. My number. Fuck me.

Damn, I wish she'd worn that to Sunny's yesterday so everyone could see her with my name on her back.

"Nice shirt," I grunted after clearing my throat and getting a grip on myself.

After slipping her shoes on, she looked back at me with a grin. "Thanks, it's my favorite Warriors shirt."

"Oh yeah?" I leaned against the counter. "Why's that?"

"Features my favorite player," she whispered, as though revealing a secret.

Despite the strange emotion swirling inside me, I shook my head. "Favorite former player."

"True." She sighed dramatically. "Which is really too bad. I sure wish I knew why he retired. It's not gonna be the same without him on the field."

Her words cut through me. I had been trying not to think about that—about how it would feel when the season started up again and I'd see all the guys running onto that field without me.

I might have my beef with the franchise and their reporters, but I'd miss the guys. Cuddy and his ridiculous pre-game ritual. Rice and his belly laugh that echoed through the locker room. All of those little things.

"You'll find a new favorite player," I said reluctantly.

"Hm." Quinn's eyes flicked over me in a way that made me feel transparent. Like she was getting closer and closer to being able to see right through me. "I'm not so sure about that. No one else rolls their eyes at me when I try to interview them."

Her words created a knot of emotion in my throat, but I swallowed past it.

"I never rolled my eyes at you during interviews."

She put her hand on her hip and cocked it to the side. "You've done it at least every day since I've been here."

"I meant back in New York."

"You were more discreet, but I caught it."

"I just don't like interviews, Castle."

She smiled reassuringly. "I know, Fletcher. That's why I've always liked you."

I raised a brow. "Pretty backward thinking for a reporter."

"What can I say? I like a challenge."

My stomach stopped somersaulting and dropped like a rock. "So what? I'm some little pet project for you?"

Her smile fell. "No, August. I just..." She took a few tentative steps toward me, and I held my breath, thinking of how my first name just left her lips and how fucking good it sounded. "I just appreciate a player who cares more for the game than for the fame. I respect all the reasons you don't want to let me in. And it makes me want to know you even more."

I wanted to argue with her. I wanted to point out what she'd said last night—that she was only coming with me this morning because it was her job. She wanted to get to know me because it was her job. But I didn't bother. We both knew it was the truth, and I didn't feel like hearing her say the words again. So instead, I cleared my throat and looked at my watch.

"We have to go. We can pick you up some breakfast on the way."

She blinked, startled by the change in conversation. But a second later, she ran with it.

"Don't worry about me. I have my trusty purse granola bar." She walked over, swiping said purse off the countertop.

I gave her an exasperated look that she seemed to understand.

"Purse snacks are the best snacks," she said with a tentative smile.

"We're stopping to get you breakfast," I said definitively. I didn't know how long we'd be at the complex today. I already felt guilty about yesterday and how she'd worked her ass off all day. I didn't need her passing out on me today.

"You're always so bossy," she muttered, but there wasn't any real heat in it.

I smirked. She didn't know the half of it. "It's a talent of mine, Castle."

Her eyes caught on mine before she flushed brilliantly, and I immediately felt better. Because even if I didn't know where the two of us stood, I knew one thing.

The way she blushed for me couldn't be fake.

It was all real.

And it was all for me.

|||

"Nice to see you again, Quinn." Finn's voice cut through the early morning air as soon as I hopped out of the jeep. Quinn, a breakfast sandwich in her stomach, had jumped out first and was already walking over to where Finn stood by the U-haul truck. "How was the rest of your night?"

I strode around the jeep and glared at my friend over Quinn's shoulder. The complex loomed behind him. It was shiny, with huge windows lining one side of the building, looking out at the ocean. We were slightly elevated compared to the main part of town, so the view was spectacular from here. Who wouldn't want to work out when they got a view like that from their treadmill?

"Good," Quinn laughed, and I frowned at how he prompted her to make that sound. I wanted to make her laugh. "I fell asleep on the way home. Woke up to August tucking me into bed."

"Aw, isn't he a sweetheart?" Finn chuckled, his amused gaze darting to mine to watch my reaction to his goading. "I hope he was a gentleman, too," he added, lips quirking.

"Is he ever not?" Quinn laughed again.

Yes. And I could show her if she wanted.

Finny struggled to keep his expression straight; he knew exactly what I was thinking. "I'm not the right person to ask." He cocked his head to the side, clearly reconsidering. "Although he did bail on our guys' night earlier this week. That was pretty fucking ungentlemanly if you ask me."

I didn't think it was possible to glare any harder, but I doubled down on the look I gave Finn.

"Fletcher." Quinn glanced over my shoulder, giving a reproving look. "How rude of you."

"I was busy," I said, clearing my throat.

"Oh yeah?" Finny hopped up onto the back of the truck. "Busy with what, Auggie?"

He was having way too much fun, and he was going to pay for it eventually. I just had to figure out the best way to fuck with him back.

"Had company," I grunted before changing the topic, not wanting Quinn to put two and two together. "The whole shipment came on the ferry?"

"Yep." Finn looked over the boxes of gym equipment and shrink-wrapped floor mats in the back of the truck. "The guys on the dock made quick work of loading it up, but I'm guessing it'll take the two of us a bit longer. I need to get the truck back to town by noon, though. My guys need it for another project."

I nodded. "Then we better get to–"

"The three of us," Quinn interrupted, and I barely swallowed a groan. Not this again.

"Castle, no." I shook my head. "You already did enough yesterday. Just hang out for a bit while Finny and I get this shit taken care of."

"You're in a time crunch. I would think another set of hands would be helpful."

"I don't want you getting hurt. We've got some heavy equipment in here, and–"

"Oh, lighten up, Auggie. I'm sure she could handle some of this stuff." To prove his point, Finn unloaded a smaller box and handed it to Quinn. "Pretty sure this one is just a bunch of deflated balls."

"I'm good at handling balls," Quinn quipped, a twinkle in her eyes as she looked over her shoulder at me. "Usually the ones I handle aren't deflated, but–"

"Castle," I groaned because I did not need to think about her handling balls. Especially balls that were not my balls.

She grinned broadly. "So where does this go?"

I sighed, feeling defeated. "Here, I'll show you."

"Bring this in while you're at it," Finny called before tossing me another light box. I caught it, shooting him a look that I was sure he understood perfectly. But he ignored it, smiling wide. "I'll be out here. I'm just gonna get as much off the truck as possible, so if anything, I can return it, and then we can get the rest inside."

"Okay, we'll be right back," Quinn said.

Finny waved us off. "Take your time!"

"Come on, Castle." I gritted my teeth as I walked toward the community sports complex entrance, wondering how much jail time I'd get for murdering my best friend.

"I know we're in a hurry today, but maybe another day you could show me around the facility," she said cheerily, hurrying to catch up with me. "It looks amazing so far."

"Sure," I said, clearing my throat. Because everything else aside, I was really proud of this place and what it was becoming. "Maybe another day."

"Or after we're done unloading the boxes?" she asked, sounding somewhat hopeful. "Unless there's something else going on today that I don't know about."

I frowned as I opened the door for her, letting her slip past me with her box of deflated balls. There was a slight touch of anxiety in her voice that I'd never really detected before, and I realized that maybe I should be better at letting her know my schedule and what was going on in my head instead of expecting her to fly by the seat of her pants all the time.

Although I hadn't really expected her to come with me today. And I hadn't expected she'd spend all day at Sunny's yesterday. But apparently, she would be connected to my hip until she got everything she needed for this article.

"Nothing else going on today, Castle." A few long strides through the front entryway, and I maneuvered in front of her, leading the way to the equipment room. "I was hoping to get in a workout later at the house, but that's it."

"Do you have a home gym?" she asked.

I opened my mouth to reply, but at that moment, all the lights in the building went out. Every single one, leaving us standing in a pitch-black hallway.

a/n:

oh no! whatever shall we do

Wattpad adding this book to a list called "a Swift touchdown" was one of the highlights of my day lol august needs to start acting a little...swifter.

xoxo amelie

fifteen | such a smartass

"FLETCHER?"

Quinn said my name hesitantly, as if expecting me to have answers as to why we were suddenly standing in the dark, but I didn't have any answers. None at all. So when she said my name the second time, panic had threaded through her voice.

"August?"

I set down what I was carrying and walked in the direction of her voice as I waited for my eyes to adjust to the dark. All of the doors to the exterior, window-filled rooms were closed, meaning the only light in the hallway was from tiny cracks beneath the doors.

"Talk to me, Castle."

"I'm over here," she said, her voice small.

Another two steps, and I ran into her, colliding with her smaller frame. Now that she was closer, I could make out the outline of her body, although just barely.

"Put down the box and take my hand," I directed.

"But I feel responsible for these deflated balls," she quipped, the panic in her voice vanishing as her body brushed against mine.

"Nothing's going to happen to your balls," I reassured, rolling my eyes to myself.

"What about your balls?" she shot back. She might not be panicked any-more, but I could tell she was still nervous, which likely explained the ridiculous shit leaving her mouth. "How are they doing?"

"We're not talking about my balls," I said flatly.

"You sure they didn't deflate a little when the lights shut off? It's okay, Fletcher. You can admit it scared you at first."

"Just put your box down," I continued, ignoring her, "and we'll come back to get them once we figure out what's going on with the lights."

"I think I know what's going on with the lights," Castle said, her voice shifting to indicate she was setting the box down. "They're not working."

"God, Castle. How come before this week, I never knew you were such a smartass?" I chuckled into the dark.

"I'm a little bit like you," she said softly, blindly jabbing my arm until she found my hand and threaded her fingers through mine. A dull heat settled in my bones, warming me. Especially when she said, "Can't let the world know too much about myself. Not unless I trust them."

I squeezed her hand, and Quinn stepped closer to me. I felt her sunshiney presence cut through the darkness, and it was so quiet that I could detect each breath she took. I shifted, feeling sucked into her. Something about the moment was calm and–

Quinn shrieked and tried to jump back, but my grip tightened, holding her hand captive.

"What was that?" she cried.

"What?"

"Something just touched my foot."

"It was probably just my foot, Castle."

"Are there mice here?" she asked, her hand jiggling in mine. I was pretty sure she was bouncing between her feet. "Of course, there are mice here," she muttered to herself. "It's a construction site."

I sighed. "I have never seen a mouse here."

"Mice are smart," she said, panic rising in her voice again. "They don't come out until they think they're alone. Trust me, they don't come scampering around my apartment until I turn off the lights. We're enemies, the mice and I."

I wasn't so sure how intelligent mice actually were, but I didn't like hearing that she was living with them. And I also didn't feel like arguing with her about it when there was a simple solution.

"Here, just–" Dropping her hand, I turned around. "Hop on my back."

"Hop on your back?" she repeated in disbelief, her voice still juggling from bouncing between two feet. "Fletcher, I don't think I could hop on your back with the lights on, let alone when I can't see you. You're like a foot taller than me."

"Fine." Before I could overthink it, I turned back around and bent down, scooped my hands behind Quinn's legs, and hoisted her into my arms. "Then I'll carry you this way."

Quinn shrieked again, but this time, there was a hint of amusement and delight mixed in there.

Or maybe that was just my wishful thinking.

I felt her wind her arms around my neck while her legs did the same thing to my waist. We felt like two puzzle pieces sliding together perfectly.

"Is that better?" I murmured in her ear, my hands tightening their grip on her thighs.

Quinn shivered.

She wasn't any more immune to me than I was to her.

"Yes," she admitted breathlessly, surprising me with the confession.

I hoisted her up higher and turned us around, beginning to walk in the direction of the front doors. Quinn clung to me, wrapping tighter around my body as though she was afraid the mice would jump up and nip at her ankles.

"How long have you lived with mice in your apartment, Castle?" I asked, keeping my voice soft.

She scoffed quietly, her breath fanning against my ear since she'd tucked her head right onto my shoulder. "The better question is, when have I ever not lived with mice in my apartment?"

"Sounds like you need an exterminator."

"Cost money," she said simply. "And I just have enough for an apartment. Not a mouse-free apartment."

I frowned into the darkness, deciding that maybe it wasn't so bad to draw out her visit here. At least she could live rodent-free in my house for a while.

"The Warriors should be paying you better," I grunted.

She laughed softly. "Tell them that."

"Maybe I will."

I felt her shake her head slightly. "Just let me finish my article about you, and I'm sure I'll get compensated well."

Great. I hated that her livelihood depended on me giving up all my secrets. I hated that even if I did give up all my secrets, it probably wouldn't help her. We were in a lose-lose situation, and I had no idea what the fuck to do about it.

"Well enough that you can hire an exterminator?"

She shrugged. "Probably."

"Are you just saying that?"

She shrugged again. "Possibly."

"You're killing me here, Castle," I groaned.

Another soft laugh came out of her at the same time I felt her fingers sift through the hair at the base of my neck. I nearly stopped walking from the shock of it, almost stumbled over my own two feet just because Quinn Castle started playing with my hair.

"How so?" she asked, and I'd be damned if there wasn't a suggestive hint in her voice. I wished I could see her face, to see if I was imagining it.

I turned my head, wondering if I could catch a glimpse of it, especially since we were nearing the doors and more and more light filtered through the hallway. But all it did was put my nose into her sweet-smelling hair and my lips in contact with her ear.

So I murmured, "You know how," and let another shiver wrack through her body.

Her fingers tugged harder on my hair, and I did falter this time. Because that tug—fuck, that tug—went straight to my dick. And while I'd been doing a pretty good job of ignoring how her body was pressed so closely to mine, how her breasts were plastered against my chest, and how her legs hugged my waist so perfectly, I couldn't ignore it anymore.

We were only a few steps from the doors, and there was no reason I couldn't put her down. We could see the floor now. We could see the sun streaming in from outside. We could see Finny unloaded shit from the truck.

I should put her down. Or I should walk her outside and then put her down. But I didn't want to do either of those things, so I turned abruptly and pressed Quinn against the wall instead.

She gasped when she made contact with the smooth drywall, which still needed a few coats of paint. Quinn's hands fell to my shoulders, holding on tight. Maybe she didn't realize how securely I had her locked in against me, but she wasn't going anywhere. My hips had her pinned, and fuck didn't that feel good.

Too good, if you asked my cock.

"August?"

Quinn pulled back, looking up at me with big, innocent eyes that I didn't believe for a second. She knew what she did to me. And if she didn't, I was about to make it abundantly clear to her. Because otherwise, I wasn't going to make it through the next week or two or however long she stayed on Evergreen Isle.

"You can't fucking play with me like that," I groaned.

Releasing one of her legs, I brought my hand to her face, pushing her hair out the way to see how her pupils constricted, and her irises sparkled when the light hit them.

Quinn's breath hitched before she ran her tongue over her bottom lip.

God, I wanted to kiss her. It would be so easy to lean in and capture those lips, to finally taste her. I've thought about it so many times over the years, but never as much as I had in the past week.

"What do you mean?" she eventually said, her voice wispy.

I rested my palm on the wall beside her face and pressed in closer, lowering my voice. "You can't make jokes about my balls and play with my hair and strip your fucking underwear off in front of me unless you–"

I bit down on my tongue as I warred with my restraint.

"Unless I...what?" Quinn asked tentatively.

Eagerly.

She wanted to know what I'd been about to say, and fuck, I wanted to tell her. But if I said every little dirty thing floating through my head right now, I was bound to scare her off. So I took a deep, steadying breath instead.

I leaned in even further, letting my lips flirt with her ear. "If you want to play, Castle, we can play. But you should know just how much I like to win."

"Oh, I know." There was a smile in her voice, and I pulled back to see it, all dazzling as she looked at me. "I've been watching you win for years, Fletcher."

A burst of pride washed over me, even if it was slightly foolish.

"You know, huh?" I countered. "So you think you know what you're doing?"

"Actually, I have no clue what I'm doing," she said, surprising me again. "I keep telling myself I'm going to stop doing what I'm doing, but I don't know how."

Shit.

She was just as hopeless as me, and I wasn't exactly sure what that meant for us.

"Fuck," I growled, dropping my forehead against hers. Our lips were only a breath away from each other, and it took everything in me not to close the distance. "Well, one of us needs to figure it out."

"I don't think it'll be me," Quinn whispered after a slight pause.

"Goddamnit, Castle." I swallowed another groan and let her drop to her feet. Slowly. "I'll tell you what you're doing. You're teasing the hell out of me. And so I need you to at least listen when I tell you to walk away. Go outside and tell Finny the lights went out. I'll be there in a minute or two."

She gave me a curious look. "What are you going to do?"

I thought that was obvious.

"Get my shit together."

In other words, get my dick to cooperate. It wouldn't be seeing any action today, and it needed to realize that.

Watching Quinn walk away with my name written across her back didn't make it easier, though. My cock throbbed as I watched her push the doors open and stride into the sunlight.

Fine.

If Quinn wanted to tease the living daylights out of me...then I suppose I'd just have to do it right back.

a/n:

poor august is about to lose it.

thanks for reading! xoxo amelie

sixteen | trouble

MY MUSCLES WERE ACHING by the time we made it back to August's house. After being on my feet all day yesterday and spending today unloading boxes, I was beat.

So when August surprisingly invited me to join him for a workout in his home gym, I declined, telling him I couldn't go another minute without rinsing off. It wasn't a lie; I badly needed a shower. But I also didn't want August to know how drained I was. He'd probably lock me up in his guest room the next time he had things to take care of around the island.

I had no idea how he had the energy to work out, but I was sure he was used to a hell of a lot more physical activity than I was. And while I certainly wouldn't mind watching August Fletcher engage in more physical activity, I figured that would be a terrible idea after what happened between us this morning.

I was already suffering from undeniable attraction to this man and making it way too obvious; watching him work out would not help my case.

Instead, I stared at the ceiling in my room and contemplated my life choices before taking a long, hot shower and wrapping myself in a fluffy robe I found folded in the bathroom. Had August put that there for me? Or did he just stock his guest bathroom as though it were a well-rated hotel? Either way, I took advantage of it.

Robe-clad with freshly blow-dried hair, I eventually emerged from my room to grab a glass of water. And when I turned the corner into the kitchen, I found a towel-wearing August Fletcher.

He didn't have a shirt on–of course, he didn't have a shirt on–and was bent over the kitchen counter as he sliced strawberries. His muscles shifted under glistening skin as he worked, hinting that he'd also just gotten out of the shower.

Never had a man looked so good while slicing strawberries.

"You must be hungry," he said, unfazed by the situation.

My mouth was watering. But it had nothing to do with being hungry. For strawberries, anyway.

When I struggled to respond, August glanced over at me. And then he did the unthinkable....he smirked.

He knew. He knew what he was doing, waltzing around without any clothes on while his hair was all wet and messy, and he smelled–ugh. Good. Too Good. And he was enjoying it. Way too much, in my opinion.

"Castle?"

"Sorry." I cleared my throat. "I'm just trying to figure out why you're standing there without clothes on."

"Does it bother you?" he asked, his eyes twinkling before he looked back at the fruit he was cutting.

"It doesn't bother me," I insisted, even though it did, in fact, bother me. In the way that seeing August Fletcher half-naked made me feel hot and bothered. Very bothered. Even more than that day we'd gone swimming, and he'd ended up in my shower wearing the same thing he had on now.

Probably because ever since then, we'd been inching closer and closer to a line that we both knew we shouldn't cross. I now had memories, real, true memories of what it felt like to have August's arousal pressed against my body, and God, I didn't know how to move on after that. I didn't know how to forget what it had felt like earlier today when I thought he would kiss me.

"Here." August, still with a smirk on his face, shoved a bowl of fruit into my hands. "Eat this while I prepare the rest of the meal. Do you like stir fry?"

"Yes." I swallowed. Hard. "Are you going to prepare it while wearing a towel?"

He lifted a brow. "I thought it didn't bother you, Castle."

"I'm just looking out for you, Fletcher," I said with a shrug, trying not to let my own smirk slide onto my face. "You have a lot of misguided faith in that towel. What happens if it falls? Looks like it wouldn't take much."

"Hmm." His eyes flicked over me, and I felt a flush rise from my neck, spreading over my cheeks and heating them. "And what happens when that belt around your waist falls? Then we'd both be in trouble, wouldn't we?"

I gaped at him for a second. There was something different about him ever since we left the athletic complex. Something more open, something more...bold.

"We definitely would be," I said breathlessly. "And you seem like a person who tries to avoid trouble."

"For the most part, I am," he allowed. "But there are things you don't know about me, Castle."

"Enlighten me," I said, taking a step forward. "After all, that's why I'm here. To learn more about you."

His expression flickered–the slightest sign of distaste for the reason I was here. I'd been noticing it more and more, every time I mentioned the article I had to produce by the end of this. But August didn't say anything about his distaste. He merely dropped his voice and murmured, "This isn't the kind of thing you can write in your article."

"Oh?" My heartbeat picked up. I could feel my skin sticking to the fuzzy fabric of my robe, a light sheen of sweat gathering on my body that I could only attribute to August. The mostly-naked, sweet-talking version of August, anyway. "And what kind of thing is it?"

"You still want to know?" he pressed. He was so close to me now that I could feel the heat radiating from his body. "Even if you can't write about it?"

I plucked a strawberry from the fruit bowl and plopped it into my mouth, slowly licking the juice off my fingers while my eyes stayed on August. His mouth pressed into a tight line as he watched me, eyes darkening.

"Yeah," I said after swallowing. "I still want to know."

I found August to be one of the most interesting men I'd ever met, and it didn't have anything to do with him being an athlete. It didn't have anything to do with my job at all. It was just so rare to find someone like him. I'd never met a man that tried so damn hard to be a gentleman.

Tried being the operative word because the way he was looking at me right now wasn't gentlemanly at all.

Yet, he hadn't acted on the things his body language told me. He hadn't admitted wanting the things his words had only hinted at.

"I shouldn't tell you," he breathed, almost like he could read my mind. He sounded dazed, as though the thoughts inside his brain were far from the words coming out of his mouth. "I really shouldn't."

"You probably also shouldn't be standing here in nothing but a towel," I pointed out, slipping another strawberry into my mouth. "But apparently, you like a little bit of trouble."

"Apparently I do," he agreed, eyes locked on my lips, "considering how much I like you."

"Oh, so I'm trouble?" I took one more strawberry before putting the bowl back on the counter.

"You're so much fucking trouble, Castle," August groaned. He ripped his attention away from my mouth, finding my gaze instead. "You have no idea."

"Give me an idea," I encouraged, stepping so close that I had to tip my head back to look at him. I winced at the twinge in my neck it caused.

"Are you okay?" August's expression immediately changed, gaze sweeping over me in concern. He retreated, making it so I wouldn't have to crank my neck to look at him. And while it was a relief for my muscles, I didn't like having space between us.

Damn.

"I think my neck and shoulders are just a little sore from unloading the truck," I said, trying to play it off.

He frowned. "You're supposed to lift with your legs, Castle."

I shrugged. "Kinda hard to do when Finny's passing things down from the truck bed."

August sighed. "Turn around."

I raised a brow at him in surprise. But when he made an impatient twirling motion with his finger, I slowly turned, unsure what he was planning.

I certainly didn't expect him to brush my hair to one side, drape it over my shoulder, and ask, "Can I touch you?"

My response came out breathless. "Yes."

August's touch gently prodded my neck as he tried to find the problem areas. Then he sank his fingers in, massaging in slow circles in the exact place I needed him. "Sore there?"

All I could manage was a whimper. "Mhm."

"Tomorrow we'll say home," he murmured, almost like a reassurance. "Rest."

"Don't change your plans for me," I argued, my eyes fluttering shut at the pure bliss spreading down my neck from where his fingers were doing their magic.

"I have a meeting, but we'll move it online," he insisted.

"Okay." I gasped when he found a particularly sensitive spot and then swallowed, trying to keep it together. "I should start putting some of my notes together and begin a draft of my article."

He hesitated. "If you have more questions about anything, I can answer them over dinner."

"Really?"

Everything about this moment felt like it must be a dream.

There was another long pause before August muttered, "I'll do my best."

And then, almost as though he was trying to wipe my mind blank of what he'd just agreed to, he dug his fingers into a pressure point, and a groan flew from my lips.

"Castle," he grunted, almost a warning.

But if he didn't want me to make a sound, then he shouldn't–

August hit another pressure point, and even though I pressed my lips together, a satisfied noise still leaked between them. Fuck, that felt good.

His hands stilled, his body leaning in. I felt his closeness, his heat. And his lips as they brushed against the back of my ear, issuing husky words. "If you keep making those sounds, I'm going to put you on the kitchen counter, spread your legs, and give you something to actually moan about."

My breath hitched, but I was prepared. I was ready to let another whimper out and wait for August to follow through on his threat. I was aching for him to follow through with his threat.

But a second later, his hands vanished, and I felt him move away.

Sure enough, when I managed to turn around despite having legs that felt like jello, August was back at the kitchen counter. This time, chopping vegetables. And all I could do was stare at him. How could he say something like that and then act like it hadn't happened?

August noticed me staring and peeked over at me. His eyes burned into mine, and his lips cocked to one side.

"Fucking trouble." He shook his head, closing his eyes as though he couldn't believe what he'd just let slip. I couldn't believe it, either. "You are fucking trouble, Castle."

We were both in trouble.

But I was starting to think that trouble could be a lot of fun.

a/n:

Who's going to crack first?

thanks for reading! xoxo amelie